Chasing: Undercover at Hedonism II

by Jason Pinaster

Other Stories by Jason Pinaster set at adult resorts:

Couples: Adventures at Hedonism II (novella)

Hedonism, Lusty Lee Log #6

Hedo II, Lusty Lee Log #7

Tantra, Lusty Lee Log 28

Blackmail Bounce

Formatting Foam

Aural Artifact

Mayan Magic

Busted Bonds

Witch's Wrath

Jason Pinaster has published numerous other erotic stories. For a **full list of his stories**, please see the back notes at page 156.

Acknowledgements: Many thanks for the suggestions from and proofreading by Sallyann Cole, Jennifer Bourgeois and Mathieu Gorman. All errors remain mine.

Author's note: All characters depicted in this work of fiction are 18 years of age or older.

Chasing: Undercover at Hedonism II

Table of Contents

Page

Chapter 1 *Jackie*

Hedonism II was reputed to be the ultimate in no-holds-barred, wall-to-wall, sex. Its erotic atmosphere was said to start right from a foyer that often included scantily-clad, if not completely nude, guests. However I wasn't in Jamaica for fun and games. I was here to take down a major international criminal. And that's why I was enduring the two-hour cab ride west from Montego Bay to Negril, on Jamaica's west coast.

The cabbie's "almost there" had made my whole body flush with excitement. But when the taxi pulled up in front of the resort's front steps, I hesitated. As soon as I started climbing up those steps, I would stop being Jennifer Logan, F.B.I special agent. Instead I would be instantly transformed into Jacqueline ("Jackie") Warne, executive secretary by day and notorious party girl by night. Halfway up the steps, a tingle of excitement rose up my body—half from the adoption of my new, and exceptionally wild identity, and half from the professional challenge I was embarking on.

Bernard Underhill was a master facilitator of all things criminal—corruption of public officials, dark websites, drugs, and worst of all, human trafficking. Some of his distant associates were involved in pedophile porn, but the extent of Underhill's involvement in this, if any, was unclear. I had been intensively studying his exploits for the past six months. Underhill had been charged several times in the past, but somehow the charges had never stuck.

However, no one is completely evil. And no one ever thinks of himself as being evil. Everyone has a motive for what they do, and that motive is always reasonable to the person. This insight was one my mentor had constantly drilled into me during the six-month preparation for this undercover assignment. If I was to get close to Underhill, I would have to think like he thinks. I would have to understand how his good qualities balanced his negative ones.

Underhill's good quality was his generosity in the bedroom.

Most men with his libido and prowess often satisfy themselves with only passing concern for their partners. Underhill was the opposite; he was more concerned with the pleasure of his lovers than with his own. One incident, well documented, had him servicing five women in one night.

Underhill might be pushing sixty, but he had apparently retained the libido he possessed when he was in his twenties. On the night in question, he had strolled down a notorious streetwalker's alley in New York, summoning an array of body types into his limo: a lithesome blonde wearing hot pants, a rotund black woman in yoga tights, a scrawny Asian, a buxom brunette and a redhead dressed up as a shiny green leprechaun.

Underhill had threaded his rather long phallus through the exceedingly generous curves of the black woman to enter her from the rear while lifting the Asian's crotch up to his mouth to eat her out. When these two women collapsed in orgiastic delight, Underhill stood the blonde and the brunette back to back. He impaled the blonde with his cock while embracing both women and using his hands to stimulate the brunette. Then he switched positions, impaling the brunette while caressing the blonde. Each time one of the women approached orgasm, he alternated. When the women were almost exhausted, he let them drop to the bed where they were so excited they brought each other off.

The kicker was the redhead. She was so frightened by the look in Underhill's eye that she stripped off her clothes and flung them at his face. But all Underhill did was laugh and proceed to take her in almost every conceivable sexual position, ultimately wracking her body with an explosive climax.

Hedonism's foyer opened directly from the steps—no door needed—and in a moment I was identifying myself as Jackie Warne to the red-shirted receptionist. As he entered Jackie's name into his computer, I inspected the light blue art deco polka dots on the wall behind him. Orange would have looked better than blue.

The receptionist flashed his bright white teeth. "I love your black hair."

I smiled back and thanked him. He was obviously just being polite, flirting by habit.

The receptionist looked down at my passport, typing away on his keyboard. "This will take awhile," he said. "Why don't you go and enjoy the buffet?" He indicated to his left, further into the resort. "There should still be some dinner left."

I glanced at my luggage and its contents of irreplaceable investigative gear.

The receptionist smiled at me. "Don't worry, your bags will be safe here."

Damn! I'd much rather be in my room downloading the latest updates from FBI headquarters. But it was important that I blend in. Calling attention to myself might imperil my operation. Still, it annoyed me to have someone else telling me what to do. I smiled, nodded and headed to the buffet while muttering curses under my breath.

Two steps into the dining room I froze. Not thirty yards in front of me was Bernard Underhill. As profiled, he was skinny and swarthy. But now he was tanned, his skin even darker. His shifty features were hidden behind a laugh. The salt air was doing him good and he looked substantially younger than his sixty years. As expected, Underhill was surrounded by a group of hangers-on, mostly young women, several with surgically-enhanced breasts. He was in a T-shirt and shorts, the women in skimpy bikinis.

There were also three men in Underhill's group. Two I recognized from the briefing notes. The new guy was pacing, constantly looking over the dining room. He must be Underhill's new head of security. He was my age, late forties. Where Underhill was tall and lanky, his security chief was of only average height. Where Underhill was thin, he was stocky. But the new guy was muscular and manly, the type of man who could break you in half without breaking a sweat. He was wearing a purple long-sleeved shirt and dark pants. He looked more than slightly overdressed until his purple shirt rustled in the breeze.

Before anyone could see me, I ducked into a restroom. I was still wearing the old pair of jeans I liked to wear while travelling and I cursed myself for not changing into shorts when we'd landed in Montego Bay. However, changing now would risk calling too much attention to myself. I settled for opening a couple of buttons on my blouse. This would allow Underhill to glimpse the tattoo that circled the top of my right breast.

I splashed water on my face and tucked my blouse tightly into my jeans. My jeans I hiked up to accentuate my hips. Even enhanced, my breasts couldn't compete with the monsters on Underhill's women. But I'd had my nipples pierced for this assignment to appeal to Underhill's kinky side. Each nipple now had a little stainless steel barbell inserted through it. Hopefully Underhill would notice the nipple jewelry through my bra and blouse.

At the buffet table, I piled my plate full of cheese, fresh fruit, jerk chicken, yams and fried rice before turning back towards Underhill and his associates.

As I walked towards them, but slightly at an angle, Underhill's new head of security was paying off the local politician who'd been profiled in my briefing notes. The politician's smile jiggled his fat. Underhill motioned to his ladies who each kissed the politician in turn. Most kissed his cheeks, but a lithe oriental beauty kissed him full on his lips. She was followed by a curvaceous black woman who not only favored him with a long kiss but also rubbed her bikini top back and forth across his chest.

The stocky security guy spotted me and his greeny eyes drilled into me. I paused, not wanting to set off any alarm bells, and made a show of looking for a seat. Underhill noticed his security chief stiffen and followed his eyes. Underhill's deep brown eyes also gave me the once over. But whereas his security chief's gaze had been clinical, Underhill's was lascivious. Butterflies flapped their wings inside my stomach.

Underhill's lips burst into a wide smile and he waved me over, motioning for the oldest of his ladies to vacate her seat for me. She gave me a dirty look, but took her plate and glass as she vacated her chair.

Underhill's eyes continued to appraise me. Sitting next to him, it was clear that he was at least the six feet his profile had pegged him at. Given that I was only five feet tall, sitting down was the best place to have our initial conversation. Even so, I felt an unpleasant twinge in my neck. He had a definite scent about him, unwashed body odor, but subtle, vaguely musky. I took a deeper whiff and felt my heart beat faster.

"What brings you to Jamaica?" he asked. His 'Jamaica' was breathless, just like a travel ad.

"Sun, sand and relaxation."

"And this particular spot?"

"I heard that Hedonism was the place for fun and games."

"And what type of *games* were you hoping to play?" His eyes sparkled.

"The type of games where I don't tell you the type of games I was hoping to play."

"So first I must ply you with alcohol?"

"Perhaps."

He looked me up and down again. "Margarita?"

My lips scrunched at the very thought of tequila.

He laughed, clearly enjoying himself. "Mojito?" Now his accent was Spanish.

"Closer."

"Dark and Stormy?"

I nodded and smiled. I preferred coke with my rum, but at least this time the rum he'd chosen was dark.

Underhill snapped his fingers in the direction of one of the waiters. "Dark and Stormy for the lady."

"Sir?" the waiter's eyes were blank.

Anger flashed across Underhill's face, but only for an instant. The waiter likely missed it. Then Underhill smiled, "Ice in a highball glass. Pour dark rum and ginger beer over the ice and garnish with a slice of lemon." He looked me up and down again. "Then add a shot of lime juice."

"Yah, Mahn!"

As soon as the waiter dashed off, Joel, Underhill's executive assistant, waved Underhill over to his laptop and Underhill was immediately and completely absorbed into it. The rest of the group chatted among themselves and I was completely alone. To hide my sudden feeling of vulnerability, I took a large bite of pineapple followed by an even larger mouthful of cheese.

The stocky security guy had his arm around the older woman who'd been seated next to Underhill when I'd strolled over. He appeared to be consoling her. I hoped I hadn't made an enemy of her. Sabotage from within could endanger my cover.

I cut another piece of pineapple, but before I could put it into my mouth, the waiter returned with my drink. The bite of the alcohol and ginger beer brought me back to center and its warmth in my belly calmed my nerves. I heard Joel's laptop slap shut and felt Underhill's body turn back towards me. I quickly swallowed the pineapple—a burst of sweetness, cold juice down my throat, syrupy pulp to chew.

"You haven't told me your name," said Underhill as he slipped into the seat next to me.

"You haven't told me yours." I relaxed a notch. The surest way to tip off a target was to show that you knew what his name was before he'd volunteered it.

"If I tell you my name, will you undo a button on your shirt?"

"Sure."

"Bernie."

"Bernie ...?"

"First the button."

I undid a button and now he could see my entire cleavage and the top of my bra. I made a show of pulling my blouse aside to allow him a clear view of the tattoo atop my right breast. "Bernie ...?"

"Another name, another button."

I nodded and undid another button, revealing even more of my bra.

"Underhill. And you are?"

"Shouldn't you be removing your shirt first?"

"You're sure?"

I nodded and filled my mouth with the rest of my cheese.

Bernie's chest was hard and flat, the type of chest which came from regular and strenuous activity and a caloric intake perfectly balanced with its owner's energy output. I gulped, both from the masculine beauty of it and from the need to clear my throat.

"Jackie," I told him. "Short for Jacqueline." I pointed to the rest of his hangers-on. "And who are your friends?"

"That requires the rest of your buttons."

"I don't know."

"Everyone will remove their shirts if you remove yours."

I raised my eyebrows while slowly and deliberately undoing the rest of the buttons on my blouse. As I untucked it from my jeans, I twisted to press my bra tight against my nipples making sure that Bernie could see the nipple pins underneath.

Bernie quickly introduced his associates, the men now shirtless. I made a show of concentrating and repeating each name, even though I already knew them. Now if I called someone by name or referred to someone by name, it wouldn't blow my cover. The new security guy was Kyle Fairbairn. Three of the women, including Angie, the slightly older one being consoled by Kyle, were white. Shaneese was black, Nara east Asian.

Bernie pointed to my drink which was still half full. "Drink up." His eyes were vaguely hypnotic.

I quickly downed the alcohol and set the glass back onto the table with a resounding thunk. "Aren't *you* going to have a drink?"

"Your beauty is intoxication enough."

"Aren't you sweet." I was pleased with how lame I sounded.

It was necessary for him to carry the conversation, for him to be taking the initiative.

"You haven't told me what kind of games you're hoping to play at Hedonism II."

"What kind of games would you recommend?"

"There's water volleyball in the pool every afternoon. Or the land-based variety if you'd prefer."

On the stage, the evening's entertainment had started. Several guests were being dared to engage in public displays of affection that would be decidedly indecent if they weren't fully clothed. I angled my head in that direction.

Bernie's eyes followed mine, then returned to my bra. "And if we were to play *that* sort of game and my body was to rub against yours, how would your nipples react?"

I batted my eyebrows and tried to look mysterious. "How do you think they would react?"

"I think they would pucker and make you gasp for air."

I shrugged. "And how would *your* nipples react?"

"Touch them and see."

In the context of the situation, I had no choice but to touch them. Bernie's lips widened as I lifted my fingers towards his chest. The sparkles in his eyes drew them all the way to his nipples. As soon as I touched them, they expanded sideways and hardened. I was the one who gasped; I had never felt a man's nipples do that before. I wanted to squeeze and caress his chest, to push my fingers into his hair, to—

But Bernie's strong hands pulled my wrists away. "My turn," he announced.

He extended his hands towards my bra and I felt a tingling. But, at that moment, the resort's professional entertainment troupe strutted to the stage with a Reggae fanfare and Bernie joined the rest of the audience in clapping. Still, I had felt my nipples engorge and my lungs tighten. These reactions had not escaped Bernie's attention. There had been something feral in his eyes as he had observed my nipples pucker and my eyes narrow in pain from the barbells pressing tight against my bra.

Tonight the resort's entertainment consisted of two muscular men lifting and twirling a voluptuous beauty about the stage. All three were Jamaican and the stage lights glistened off the oil on their black bodies. Their routine didn't involve as much touching as the guests had engaged in but its artistry made their movements much more suggestive.

Bernie put his arm around my shoulder and brought his other hand in front of my breast. My blood rushed towards his fingers even though they were at least an inch away from my bra.

"Is this the type of game you had in mind?"

I nodded. I didn't trust my tongue.

The routine ended. Once again, Bernie broke physical contact to clap and I could breathe again. A new pair of performers strutted onto the stage. The male was wearing a white suit, white shirt and white tie, his outfit exotic against his ebony skin. The female wore a red skirt and pink blouse. Her skin was lighter than his. She strutted around the stage until he pulled a riding crop from behind his back and slapped it against his hand.

"Or is this the type of game you had in mind?" asked Bernie.

"What's the game?"

"She gives herself over to him completely so that he can pleasure every particle of her being."

On stage, white suit slapped his riding crop against his thigh. She undid the top button of her blouse. Slap! She undid another button. Slap! Slap! Slap! Soon all her buttons were undone. Slap! She let her blouse fall down behind her. Bernie's hand was warm atop my knee.

On stage, her bra was white lace and I could see the outline of an even darker nipple against her light brown skin. He slapped his crop against his palm. Her hands went to the clasp on her skirt. One more slap and the skirt fell to the stage revealing a skimpy white lace thong. Bernie's hand was most of the way up my thigh. Half of me was apprehensive—this was moving way too fast. The other half urged Bernie's hand higher.

On stage, she held her hand out for the riding crop and he reluctantly handed it over. She moved around behind him and pulled his jacket to the floor.

I leaned over to whisper to Bernie. "I thought you said that *she* was giving herself over to *him*." His arm was electric against the side of my breast.

"A game is never what it seems."

I leaned back and breathed. On stage, the woman tapped the handle of the riding crop against each of the buttons on his shirt and he immediately undid each button she tapped. She again went behind him and pulled his shirt to the floor. Now only his white tie protected his chest. Bernie's hand gave my jeans a gentle squeeze, rippling a jolt up my spine.

On stage, she strutted around in front of him and waved the crop up and down the length of his zipper. His pants immediately dropped to the floor. For a moment I thought he was nude. Then, as he turned, I could just make out a thin tight thong almost exactly matching his skin both in color and in sheen. Bernie's hand was at the top of my thigh, the side of his hand pressing lightly against my crotch. But even through two layers of clothing, the heat from his hand penetrated deep inside.

Bernie smiled. "And how do you like this game?"

"The one on stage or the one your hand is playing between my legs?"

"Aren't they the same game?" He vibrated his hand and smiled as my breath caught in mid inhalation.

The female performer grabbed her partner's tie, pulled his lips to hers, and gave him a full kiss. At first their large lips were barely touching, then they pressed tight and we could tell that her tongue had slithered into his mouth. She let go of the tie and pushed him back. He stood, startled and breathless. Bernie's hand began to move up and down, sliding my jeans against my panties. The heat inside my sex was out of all proportion to the subtle movements of his hands. I gasped. He smiled.

Bernie bent to my ear. This time I turned towards him and felt my nipple barbell twist gently against his arm. "And the game," he breathed, "is the fun in playing the game or how it ends?"

"It's how the game is played."

On stage, she was hitting his legs with the crop, mostly on the outside of his thighs, but when she struck between his legs, his crotch seemed to swell. Bernie moved his hand back and forth and I felt a drop of moisture loosen my pussy lips.

Bernie rippled the muscles in his arm and I suddenly realized that my barbell was still pressed against him. Had he felt it?! I pulled back, aghast.

"Jackie?" His voice was soft and deep.

"Bernie?"

"I like the way you say my name."

On stage, the riding crop seemed to touch his thong. He moved back, horrified, his hands in front of his crotch. She flung the riding crop aside and advanced, her hands intent on grabbing what he was protecting. His back hit the side of the stage. She took a step forward and waved at his hands. He reluctantly removed his hands from the front of his crotch. His thong glistened in the light. She licked her lips.

I felt Bernie lean towards me. "Play the game well, Jackie, and you might like the ending even more."

On stage, she grabbed for his crotch. But he slid away and escaped through the curtains at the back of the stage. She ran after him. Bernie removed his hand. We clapped and clapped as I heaved oxygen into my lungs.

As the applause died, a resort porter arrived, pulling my luggage. "Jacqueline Warne?" he asked.

"Jacqueline *Warne*," repeated Bernie, his voice triumphant with the unearned information.

I looked at my luggage, then at Bernie. "And how does this development play into your game?"

"Any amateur can respond to an obvious move, a pro knows how to react to the subtle ones." His pronunciation of 'amateur' and 'subtle' had an English accent.

"Subtle ones?"

He nodded, his face serious, but his eyes sparkling. "For example, if you'd said 'good night' you would have forced me to choose between letting you go, asking to see you again at another time or trying to come to your room tonight."

"But…?"

The porter had turned to go and I had to shuffle after him, turning back and forth between the clickety-clack of my retreating luggage and Bernard Underhill.

"But you said nothing," he continued. "The next move is still up to me, but I won't risk being called out of bounds if I ask to come to your room."

"Very good. So what is your move, *Bernard*?" I was now a good ten feet away from him.

He walked briskly towards me. "My *move* is to follow you and see what you do."

I hurried after the porter and caught up to my luggage. In a moment Bernie was beside me. Not quite touching, but very, very close. My luggage, full of important data and surveillance equipment, not to mention an unauthorized pistol, swayed back and forth in front of us as it clattered along the pathway.

In a few moments, the porter was lifting my luggage up the stairs and my attention continued to be divided between its contents and Bernie who was being a gentleman and helping me up the stairs.

One door down, the porter opened the door to my room, handed me the keycard and lifted my luggage inside. Bernie paused at the door, forcing me to choose between saying good night with him still outside or ushering him inside. Damn, the man was pushy. My hormones made the choice for me and I waved him over the threshold.

Inside the room, the porter described the controls to the air conditioner, showed me how to operate the shower, and demonstrated entering a code into the safe in the closet. He angled his head towards Bernie, "Enjoy your stay, pretty lady."

I fumbled in my purse and came out with a five-dollar bill that I extended towards him.

But he shook his head, "No tipping at Hedo."

And then he was gone. The door clicked shut. I was alone with Bernard Underhill. Do or die. I pointed to the shower. "I should freshen up."

"No need." He stepped towards me.

I backed towards the wall, not avoiding Bernie, rather following his lead. My back touched the wall. Bernie's body touched mine. His heat made me warm all over. Long hands reached behind me. His mouth bent towards mine. Lips soft and warm, then hot, hard, demanding. Mine responded, demanding him. My bra was tight then loose.

He stepped back. I was still warm, but his heat had left me. He flung my bra aside and admired my breasts. Two fingers reached forward and flicked my nipple piercings. Hot lightning drew all my breath into my breasts. His hands caressed my breasts, flooding my lungs with air. Again he flicked my nipple jewelry and again I was breathless. But this time my sex and my stomach were also drawn up to his fingers.

I was barely standing, grateful for the support of the wall, wondering when I would breathe again as Bernie, slowly, tortuously undid the button to my jeans and unzipped them. They slipped slowly down my thighs.

"Breathe," he whispered and I gasped air into my lungs. He kissed me lightly, stepped back, and dropped his own jeans to the floor. His briefs, black shiny spandex, swiftly followed and Bernard Underhill was standing nude in front of me. He was skinny, pure hard muscle. His hands waved in the air, following the curves of my body, but not touching, his movements fluid like a cat. A thin coating of hair covered his body in a layer of delicate silk. His erection was enormous.

Bernie pointed to my panties. "What shall we do with these?"

I glanced down at them. They were cotton, well-worn and ordinary. After a long day of travel, I had planned to throw them away.

But Bernie had more creative ideas. "I could rip them off your body." Yikes! "Or I could caress them until they're saturated with womanly juices." My pussy liked *that* idea. "Or I could lift them tight into your slit and pull them from side to side." Even *better*! "Or—"

"Lift and pull."

My panties stretched tight into my vulva, then back and forth, brushing against my pussy lips, then between where she was hot and wet. Bernie had one hand on the front of my panties, the other on their back pulling the thin cotton into the middle of my buttocks.

His lips were on my neck, almost all the way behind my ear. "Should we make her come, just like this?"

"Yes." His front hand began to vibrate, sending a tingle back to the bottom of my spine. "No!" My hands shot to his cock. He was round and wide and *hot*!

"Don't worry, you can have him too."

"No…" But my voice melted, surrendering to his demands.

His hand moved the thin cotton back and forth, sliding up and down my pussy lips, flicking this way and that against my clit. I felt my climax begin to gather deep within, to squeeze and knead my womb.

The vibrations in his hand suddenly changed. His lips kissed the back of my neck, then withdrew, his breath tingling down my spine. "Now!" he whispered. Below his grip was firm and gentle— back and forth, up and down, vibrating all at once. His lips brushed the back of my spine.

My climax exploded from my drenched panties, up my spine and into his lips. Then spasm after hot spasm tightened my sex, drawing my entire being into her roiling ecstasy. I shut my eyes and let it go on forever.

When I could see again, I was nude, spread-eagled on the bed, and staring up into the mirror on the ceiling. Half the mirror was covered by Bernie's back. Then there was the bed and my luggage. I suddenly needed to get into my luggage, to file a report, to—

"Are you ready?" he asked.

His erection, very hot and very hard, was pressing against my very relaxed opening. "But I already came." Selfish of me, I know, but Bernie was somehow drawing out the first thought that was coming to mind.

"You can come again."

"But I never—"

He slipped inside quickly, nothing special there. But the way he filled me, that *was* special. He pressed against my womb, firmly caressing it. He stroked back and forth against *all* the pleasure spots inside me. His shaft stroked pleasure along my pussy lips. And each time our pubic bones touched, he moved in a different direction pulling unique sizzles into my clit.

In the mirror, each of Bernie's vertebrae shifted in sequence, like a well-oiled engine. His butt muscles clenched and released with omnipotent power, pumping heat inside and pulling juices out.

I began to feel excited again, but I shook the idea out of my head. This was all about Bernie. I'd already had my fun. I wouldn't have another orgasm until I'd had a good night's sleep. I squeezed my pussy, urging him to climax. I needed to get him out of my room, to file my reports, to—

But there it was again, arousal unmistakable and urgent. Little frissons of excitement all along his sliding shaft. The sensations on my pussy lips joining and uniting with those in my clit. My clit pulsed deep inside. The orgasm was small, mild, so I was able to taste every quiver squeezing and releasing inside me. I'd never tasted anything so sweet and delicate. It was even more special than the usual overpowering spasms.

Friends had talked about multiple orgasms, but this had been my first. It'd been nice, but hardly the peak experience they'd described. I'd had my pleasure. Twice! Now it was Bernie's turn. "Harder!" I urged him.

"What's your rush?"

"I—"

Yet again. Sexual excitement was building within me for a *third* time. Surely I couldn't come *again*?!

"Hard or soft?"

"You're hard! And hot! Harder, Bernie, *harder*."

But he didn't alter his strokes. In all the way. Then his shaft pulled out until just the tip of his cock was inside me. Then down until our pubic bones touched. Bones rotating together. A steady rhythm, with just enough variation to keep our nerves interested. His power penetrated deep into my womb.

"Harder!" I begged.

But he shook his head. "More little ones or another big one?"

His butt pumped away, obviously in no hurry. I, on the other hand, needed to get into my suitcases. "This should be *your* turn."

"This *is* my turn."

"I—"

Two short sharp thrusts from Bernie's cock confirmed that I was once again in the grip of sexual excitation. "Small or large?" he demanded.

An odd question, given the size of what was in me. But he was referring to my orgasm, not himself. "Large." It was time to see what my friends had been talking about.

He pumped me back up the mountain. I didn't have to do anything. His hand on my butt was holding me so tightly that I *couldn't* do anything. Each thrust wound the spring inside me tighter and tighter. There was a spasm. But not orgasm, it was the spring being wound tighter than it'd ever been wound before. Then another.

"Bernie," I begged. "Now!"

But he shook his head, the sparkles in his eyes glorying in their utter and complete dominion over me.

Another spasm. "No!" I yelled.

Only then did he remove his hand from my butt and alter his strokes. Slow and short, balancing me perfectly atop the cusp of the mountain. "Are you ready?" he asked.

"Yes!" I gasped.

"Hard or soft?" Bernie's lips smirked. He knew he was torturing me.

"Hard!" I yelled, taking a measure of revenge by digging my nails into his back.

He slammed his cock into me, throwing my arms off his back. I held onto the sheets for dear life. He sucked my stomach out with his cock. I tried but failed to brace myself. His next thrust pushed me over the edge then cruelly sucked me back. But mercifully his next thrust pushed me all the way over the edge and I broke free from his grip.

My muscles were slack from all this activity. Even so, the spasms wrenched them tight between my pelvis, up my spine and down into my toes. This time I felt every contraction and release. My eyes fluttered, but didn't shut fully. I was warm and wonderful and floating atop wave after wave of divine pleasure. Electricity quivered up and down my pussy lips. The back of my neck shivered. My lungs vibrated in harmony with universal rhythms. My heart beat love—love for me, love for Bernie, and just plain love. The spasms and vibrations began to weaken, but I lingered, tasting the edges of each and every one.

Bernie pulled himself off me and kissed my forehead. I couldn't move. Sunlight was streaming in through the window. I felt him move away. Two heartbeats and far away a door clicked shut.

An eternity later, as I unpacked, I reflected on my progress so far. I had gotten close to Underhill and it would be only natural for me to visit his group. I had yet to gather much in the way of evidence of Underhill's criminality, but one thing I could corroborate: Bernard Underhill was *some* lover!

Equally important, I had had experienced Bernie's charisma up close and personal. I would have to be on guard against it in the future.

I removed my sidearm from the special packaging which had allowed it to evade customs. A quick check ensured that the clip was full of bullets and that there was a round in the chamber. My eyelids shut and I had to shake my head to remain awake. I struggled to jot down a few thoughts. A more formal report would have to wait until the morning.

Chapter 2 *Kyle*

I had to use an idiosyncratic system for my notes in case Underhill or Joel Ritchie, his right-hand-man, discovered them. Anyone ignorant of my intent would think I was typing a novel. So I described my bribe to the politician the night before as inserting bait to catch a big fat Grouper. I made a mental note of the corrupt official's face on the body of the big fat fish so that I'd be able to transcribe all the details later.

When I'd first caught sight of Jacqueline Warne, all sorts of alarm bells had gone off. Her long black hair framed an attractive face that lit up when she smiled. And her curves stirred reactions below my belt line which were inappropriate to the task at hand. But what had set off the alarm bells was the quiet confidence with which she moved. It was the confidence of someone skilled in more than one martial art, something out of place in Hedo's relaxed decadence.

And of course, Underhill had seen where I was looking and had waved her over.

The predicable flirting had followed. Partway through, their chit-chat had led to introductions. The conversation had flowed organically, but still, Jackie now knew the names of Underhill's entire entourage. Me, she knew only by my alias, Kyle Fairbairn. But still…

This morning, I'd divided my attention between typing my 'novel', staking out the corner of the dining room favoured by Underhill, grabbing the occasional bite from the buffet, strolling over to Warne's room and proofreading my typing.

As usual, Joel, Underhill's beady-eyed nerd of an assistant, had been the first to arrive to greet the sunrise. He cracked open his laptop, rapidly entered the series of keystrokes which I knew to be his ever-changing password, and began to open and scroll through several items.

"Any cyber security flags?" I asked.

"If there were, I'd tell you."

"You have fun last night?"

His smile answered my question. His eyes told me to mind my own business.

Joel typed some more while I strolled over to see if the pineapple plate had been freshened. When I returned, he shut the lid to his laptop. "Watch this."

My eyes flicked back and forth between Joel's retreating form and his laptop. I wished that my laptop were as capable as his. But the first time Joel had seen my laptop, he'd torn it apart to ensure that it had no internet connection. Since then, as long as I made no secret of using it, my laptop sailed under his radar.

It was on one of my trips towards Warne's room when I met Underhill ambling towards me, a wide grin on his face. "You look pleased with the world," I told him.

"Irie, Man."

"Irie?" Irie was Jamaican for everything is alright, better than alright.

His grin went even wider. "All I had to do was pull her panties into her slit and Jackie came. She has this freaky lizard tattoo, it's tail looping around her right tit, then down her ribs, its belly on top of hers and its snout sniffing her cunt. Her tits are pierced. And very sensitive. I flicked the piercing and she felt it all the way down into her cunt. Then I grabbed onto her juicy handful of an ass and fucked her silly until she begged me to let her come, then I fucked her some more."

"Sounds like you had a good time," I told him. Jacqueline Warne was *definitely* going to be a problem.

"The best. You haven't got laid since we arrived, have you?"

"Boss, I can't watch over you if I'm plowing—"

"Nonsense. You need a good fucking. It'll make you relaxed. Keep you sharp."

I nodded but did my best to look skeptical.

Underhill shook his head. "Don't give me that look. Take Jackie. Take Angie. Show them a good time."

He was trying to be generous. But he was also treating the women as possessions. I couldn't tell what was worse and decided to change the subject. "Do you want me to do a background check on Miss Warne?"

He smiled again and shook his head. "She's here on vacation. She wants to escape the hypocrisy. After last night's fuck, no one else will ever be good enough. End of story."

I cursed under my breath. I needed to check her out. And Underhill's was the only database I had access to at the moment. As we entered the dining room, I looked longingly at the computer Joel was typing into.

While Underhill huddled with Joel over their laptop and

munched on the plate of fruit and muffins brought over to him by Angie, I went back to my 'novel'. Angie's role had started to increase in prominence. If I could gain her confidence, she might fill in some of the blanks in my investigation.

Last night, after Underhill had left with Jacqueline Warne, I'd sat down with Angie, brushed her brunette hair away from her face, and we'd shared our childhood fears and dreams. At least I hoped that they were Angie's actual fears and dreams. Kyle's were quite different than my own. I'd told her I'd wanted to be an astronaut. She'd wanted a large family.

But Underhill continued to be the main character in my encrypted narrative. I could testify as to his corruption of the fat grouper, but I had no corroborating evidence. Certainly nothing which would trigger the interest of my superiors at the Royal Canadian Mounted Police. It was clear that Underhill was heavily involved in drug trafficking and I was keeping my eyes open for hard evidence. But enforcing prohibition didn't turn my crank and besides charging Underhill with a drugs offence would be repeating what had been done to Al Capone—putting a mass murderer away for tax evasion. What I really wanted to do was to shut down Underhill's human trafficking network, especially the tentacles engaged in trafficking children.

Over at their laptop, Underhill and Joel pointed at the screen and congratulated themselves. I wished that I could go over and smash the laptop and feed them its pieces until they suffocated. But that would leave the network intact.

Like Angie, I was a supporting character in my novel. Everyone back north thought that I was on long-term medical leave pending the investigation of several of my more exuberant escapades. If the supervening conduct authority had its way, I'd be brought up for a hearing which would result in my long-term leave being made permanent. And it wouldn't be for medical reasons.

On the laptop, Joel was having a video chat. Underhill had positioned himself off to one side, out of view of the camera. Joel was discussing the weather in detail, both here and in New York. Underhill made a cutting motion across his throat. "Even sunshine must end," Joel told the person on the other end.

I suddenly wished I wasn't operating without a safety net. Only one person back home, a friend and former colleague, knew what I was up to. He'd retired last year but was still on good terms with several current R.C.M.P. officers who, unlike me, were still in good standing. However, as a former member of the force, he had only very limited access to police resources. But his extensive undercover experience had helped us document my clandestine identity. So far 'Kyle Fairbairn' was holding up.

The whole operation was highly risky, but if I could bring Underhill down, it would be worth it. One exceptionally bad guy and more than a few of his minions in jail would be worth risking a couple more black marks on my record. If Underhill were arrested, I might even be restored to full operational status. As far as Underhill knew, I had a deep dark criminal past. The cold-case murder we'd pinned on Kyle Fairbairn had been the *pièce de résistance*. But if Underhill ever got even a whiff that I'd been with law enforcement, I'd be dead before I could draw my next breath.

By lunchtime, Underhill had apparently finished with business and he shut the cover to the laptop. His whole entourage joined him in a lavish feast, plate after plate coming in from the buffet. In addition to Joel, there was one other man. As best as I could tell, pug-faced Johnny was a low-level go-fer. Angie was the oldest of the five women. The other two white women were young and flighty but Underhill seemed to keep them around because they had large breasts and were generally appreciative. Shaneese, her skin a dark *café au lait*, had a quick wit and a calming demeanour. Nara, who I'd pegged as Japanese, was highly intelligent and intensely devoted to Underhill. She was the only one without burgeoning breasts.

Partway through lunch, the resentment towards Jackie bubbled to the surface. Angie had tried, but failed, to defuse their anger.

"You're jealous!" joshed Underhill.

His attempt at humour just made the younger white women all the angrier.

Angie held up her hand to quiet her companions, then turned to Underhill. "We do so much for you, it's not fair that she just strolls in and gets to spend *all night* with you."

Underhill set his knife and fork down on his plate. The entire table went silent. He looked straight at the young white woman who'd been the most vociferous. "So you think I should make it up to you?"

She hesitated, then finally said, "Yes." Angie and all the

other women joined in a chorus of agreement.

Underhill held up a hand and there was immediate silence. "How about a role-play?" he asked.

The ladies excitedly agreed. The men nodded. From what I'd gathered, these role-plays generally devolved into an orgy and everyone got laid.

"I'll be President Trump," announced Underhill.

"I'll be Melania," chimed in Angie.

But Underhill shook his head. "Kyle will be security, you can keep him company." Angie was clearly downcast, but, as a good and loyal trouper, she looked at me and shrugged her shoulders. I smiled back at her, pleased with another opportunity to chat her up and assess whether she'd inform on Underhill if push came to shove.

At Underhill's instruction, I scooted off to the front desk to reserve the Romping Room for his proposed role-play. By day, the room, really an open-air courtyard, was used by the spa. After the evening show, it was turned over to whichever guests wanted to engage in exhibitions of public sex.

With a little cajoling and a promise to support a local charity, the manager agreed to let us have the Romping Room to ourselves for an hour and half at the end of the evening meal.

After an early dinner, we decamped to the Romping Room. Underhill sat at the head of the table and motioned for everyone else to take their seats. "I will be the President," he proclaimed. "Everyone else is an Apprentice. Do what I say, and do it well, you will be moved up the table. Fail, and you go to the bottom."

Being security meant that I'd wander around the Romping Room, sometimes in, sometimes outside, in a random fashion. The strength of this method was varying my distance from Underhill and his entourage to make sure that no one was keeping him under surveillance. The fact that I had managed to allow Underhill to think that it was his idea was icing on the cake.

As I checked the periphery inside, Underhill came up with his first test. "Shaneese, plug your ears." As soon as she complied, he pointed to Joel. "Mr. Ritchie, you will give her a bath. You will succeed if you can make her say 'heavenly'."

Joel took Shaneese by the wrist. "Time for a bath," he told her as he led her to the largest of the three spa pools and positioned her under the water falling down from the ceiling at the back. Her bright blue bikini, once wet, became almost translucent allowing me a glorious view of her all-natural mammaries and the outline of her nipples. One of the other women scampered inside the washroom and came back with a bar of soap which she handed to Joel.

Shaneese turned her back to Joel and he began to work up a generous lather. "How's this?" he asked.

"Lovely."

He turned her around and lathered her tummy. "And this?"

Shaneese looked back at the table and the seven pairs of eyes awaiting her response. She began to understand that her responses had something to do with Joel's assigned task. "Wonderful?"

Underhill shook his head and now Shaneese fully understood the dance that President Underhill was choreographing. She jutted her breasts forward and the sight of her nipples trying to poke through her swimsuit made me stumble.

Joel reached the soap towards her bikini top but she shook her head and pulled her breasts back. "The soap will leave little white marks." When Joel put the soap down on the side of the pool, she jutted her breasts forward again. He reached forward to undo the clasp on her back while she playfully rubbed herself against him. Underhill clapped. Everyone else cheered.

Joel lathered her left breast. It was round and firm, but also soft where the soap touched.

The white soap on Shaneese's dark skin *was* heavenly, but she described it as merely "Glorious."

The bar of soap traced an even more sensuous pattern around her right nipple which was even blacker than the rest of her. The little bud stood tall and proud in response to his attentions. "Uhhhh," she moaned when he slid the soap across her nipple.

"A verbal response is required," chided Joel.

"Spectacular?"

He shook his head and lathered her tummy.

"Lovely."

Joel's shoulders slumped.

Shaneese slid her bikini bottom beneath the water and used her feet to pull it the rest of the way off. She turned to Joel and extended her ripe round rump towards the bar of soap in his right hand. He worked up an inch-high lather.

"Stupendous?" she offered.

Joel shook his head, defeated.

Shaneese dipped her bum below the water. When she stood, she smiled at him. "Don't give up." She pointed to the rich black forest of curls between her thighs. "She likes you, Joel." Shaneese indicated the spot where her fur vanished between her thighs. "She's never let me down yet."

Joel shrugged. What did he have to lose? He slid the bar of soap deep into the forest, a white interloper exploring deepest darkest Africa.

"Heavenly," she moaned when he brought the soap forward.

"Joel, my man!" enthused Underhill. Everyone else on the table was glum as Joel and Shaneese slid into the places of honour next to Underhill.

I left to go outside. My random patrol method had the added benefit of allowing me to avoid participation in the outrageous orgy about to unfold. It would also allow me to chat intermittently with Angie who had positioned herself at a table a short distance from the Romping Room door. I circled left around the outside perimeter and headed towards the dining room bar.

On my way back, I brought Angie a Jamaican Kiss, her favorite drink. It was similar to a White Russian but with light rum instead of vodka. I'd had the bartender add an extra shot of rum in the hopes of loosening her up.

She took a sip and angled her head towards the door. "What's happening in there?"

"The usual touch and grab. Why is Mr. Underhill making you sit this one out?"

"He likes them young, I guess." She took a long draw of her Jamaican Kiss.

"How long have you been with him?"

"A couple of years." Interesting. Our intelligence reports indicated that the average tenure of a woman in Underhill's entourage was measured in months, not years. And the reports had indicated that Angie had joined only a little more than a year ago.

"How did you meet him?" I asked.

"I was working behind the desk at a hotel. Joel was doing the registration. Bernie's eyes were boring into me and I couldn't take *my* eyes off him. Joel became impatient which seemed to amuse Mister Underhill. Bernie asked me out. When Bernie's group checked out of the hotel a week later, so did I."

"So you've been with him the longest?"

She shook her head. "Technically Nara has been with him longest. She used to work with one of his businesses. She's been travelling with us for about the last three months."

"Shaneese seems to go everywhere with her." Ordinarily pressing for this much detail might be risky, but Angie appeared to be concentrating on her drink.

"Shaneese was Nara's friend. They came together."

I slid down to sit beside her. "Maybe after the role-play is over, you and I could take a walk down by the beach?"

She shook her head. "I have to stay here in case Bernie needs something." I kicked myself and wished I'd been smoother. But clearly she wasn't ready to assist in my investigation.

I stood up, kissed her on the top of her head, and re-entered the Romping Room.

Inside, four couples were on the mattresses which were on the floor in the corner. It was obviously some sort of oral sex competition. Joel, Shaneese, and Johnny the bent-nosed go-fer were receiving head. Nara and two other white women were kneeling in front, bestowing the honours.

"Go, girl!" encouraged Joel.

"Flick my clit!" shouted Shaneese.

Johnny leaned back, shut his eyes and enjoyed his blowjob in silence.

"Thirty seconds," proclaimed Underhill.

The women on the floor redoubled their efforts. Shaneese received a sideways back-and-forth motion while Joel got extra sucking. Shaneese moaned. Joel yelped. Loud slurping noises slithered up and down Johnny's penis and his eyes flashed open, wider than wide. I felt a stirring in my pants.

Nara slowly brought her mouth up to the tip of Joel's penis. His fists gathered the sheets. She held her mouth open and plunged down his length. He relaxed and she slowly brought her mouth back up to the tip of his penis, obviously maintaining suction. At the tip, she rocked her head back and forth. He had the sheets in his fists again, but not as tight. She plunged her head down his pole, but this time her lips were clamped tight around his penis. "Shit!" shouted Joel.

Underhill clapped his hands. "Time!"

The kneeling women stood. Nara licked her lips. Those laying on the mattresses shuffled backward and slowly scrambled to their feet. Protuberances at pelvis level made this more difficult for the men.

"Anyone come?" asked Underhill.

Joel raised his hand. He and Nara were ensconced next to Underhill at the head of the table.

Underhill made a show of teasing his assembled multitude with the next test and I took the opportunity to exit the room. As I passed Angie, I noticed that she'd finished her drink. "Another?" I asked.

She nodded her head.

A few moments later, satisfied that no one was unduly interested in Underhill or in breaching the Romping Room, I set another Jamaican Kiss down in front of Angie. She quickly drained half the glass.

"Thirsty?" I asked.

"Bored."

"Ready for that walk on the beach?"

She nodded and took another sip. I angled my head towards the door of the Romping Room, indicating I'd do a quick check before we set out for the beach. I stood, unlocked the door and stepped back inside.

The room was empty. No one at the table! I dashed madly around. What the hell happened? Where was Underhill?! He'd have my balls for this! But then I heard a thwack from one of the side rooms and a plaintive "Ow!" from Johnny's mouth. I raced over and threw the door open.

Johnny was attached, spread-eagled, to an 'X'-shaped cross. Underhill's two white women were standing beside the go-fer and alternatively pinching or biting his nipples. Nara and Shaneese were taking turns whipping his erection with a cat-of-nine-tails. Johnny's penis was reddish but quite hard and he seemed to be enjoying himself. As each woman finished swatting his privates, she passed the whip on to the next.

Underhill and Joel were standing off to one side.

"Everything's okay," I told Underhill.

He nodded and went back to watching the torture being visited upon his go-fer. Nara, the thin Japanese woman, delivered a particularly vicious strike but this time Johnny managed to stifle his cry.

"What's the game?" I asked Joel.

"The woman who elicits the strongest reactions from Johnny wins. He gets points for maintaining his hard-on and for showing *some* reactions but for being able to restrain himself from showing *strong* reactions."

Shaneese used the handle of the whip to tap Johnny's balls. His eyes bugged out and he groaned. She had a satisfied look on her face when she passed the whip to one of the white women.

To my right was a glassed-in shower. Further down, the wall at the end of the room was wall-to-wall mirror. Several mattresses were placed against the far wall. Beside the X-shaped cross, several chains dangled from the ceiling. Two-thirds of the long wall were covered in plush purple velvet. Where we were, the walls were blood red. If this wasn't the epitome of kinky, I had no idea what was.

The buxom redhead who'd been alternating between sucking and biting the go-fer's right tit wrapped the strands of the whip around Johnny's penis and began to slide it up and down his pole. "Come for me, Johnny boy."

Johnny shuddered. Obviously part of him wanted to comply with her suggestion.

She reached under the sliding whip and caressed his balls. "Come on, Johnny, you know you want to."

"She's not allowed to use her hands," protested Shaneese.

Underhill clapped his hands. "Next!"

The redhead pouted and handed the whip to her tit-torturing mate, an equally buxom blonde who wrapped the whip's strands around Johnny's gonads. "The twisting stops when you cry my name," she told him. She began to twist.

"Mr. Underhill! That's not fair!" protested Johnny.

Underhill shrugged and smiled, obviously enjoying the spectacle.

"No, please!" yelped Johnny. The discomfort in his voice was palpable.

The blonde twisted some more. "All you have to do is say 'Lydia'." Her eyes were as cold as ice.

Johnny bit his lip. She continued to twist the whip, but slower now. Johnny gasped.

"Ready to say my name?" She gave a jerking twist.

He shook his head. She twisted and pulled at the same time.

"Lydia!" he cried.

She let go of the whip. Triumph flashed in her eyes, but her lips pouted at having been deprived of more fun. The whip slowly unwound, then dropped to the floor.

Underhill clapped his hands. "Bravo!" Everyone clapped. "Back to the table," he said. "It's time for the last round."

Everyone started to shuffle back into the main courtyard of the Romping Room so I slipped outside and locked the door behind me. Angie was just finishing her drink. I did a quick perimeter check, then returned to Angie. "I think they're about to finish up," I told her. She got up and we went inside. Regrettably Underhill's grand finale was of more interest to her than a stroll on the beach with me.

The women—all four of them—were nude and kneeling forward doggie-style on the mattresses in the center of the room, their fingers intertwined at the tops of their heads. Their knees were spread and their bums wiggling. I watched transfixed as Joel and Johnny penetrated each of them in turn. Sometimes they lingered for a few thrusts, sometimes they were in and out. Moisture glistened on their poles.

Angie nudged me and I remembered that I was supposed to lock the door.

As soon as I turned around, Underhill waved us over. "The women who keeps their interest the longest win."

"What do they win?" asked Angie.

"The two with the highest score spend the night with me."

Angie began to unbutton her blouse. "Shouldn't I get a chance too?" she asked.

Underhill shook his head. "You keep Kyle company."

I did some quick math. That would leave one woman each left over for Johnny and Joel.

On the mattresses, the two underlings were thrusting themselves into the two white women, their hands on the women's hips. The women were moaning, obviously enjoying themselves. The redhead reached behind towards Joel's balls and he adjusted his knees to facilitate her efforts. The woman beneath Johnny followed suit. The two men groaned in appreciation and began to float.

"No hands!" shouted Shaneese.

"No hands!" confirmed Underhill.

The men reluctantly pushed the women forward and they landed flat on their breasts. The women quickly scrambled back to their knees, bums thrust high in invitation.

But Joel had moved on to Shaneese, Johnny to Nara. The men glanced back at the two white women, obviously wanting to return to them as quickly as possible. But Shaneese began to rock and thrust her hips, capturing Joel's full attention. Nara lifted her knees off the mattress every time Johnny thrust forward. His responding grunts indicated that he was being sucked deeper into a woman than he'd ever been sucked before. Judging from their movements, the men were about to climax.

Underhill clapped his hands three times and everyone stood. The women all ran to Underhill, attempting to influence his verdict. A veritable United Nations. The women fondled and kissed Underhill. Ultimately, he gathered the blonde and the Japanese women in his arms and waved the black and redheaded women over to his underlings.

But the redhead, who'd ended up next to Johnny, pointed to Nara, the thin Japanese. "I'm better than *her*!

Underhill tried to turn away.

"The boss gets to decide," Johnny told her, putting a hand on her shoulder.

The redhead shoved Johnny's hand aside, put her hands on her hips, took a deep breath and jutted her extremely ample breasts towards Underhill. "I'm better than *her*!"

"What you are is fired," Underhill told her.

"But the role-play—"

"Not from the role-play, from the group." Underhill's eyes flashed savage anger. "Now, clear out of your room and leave the resort."

The redhead hesitated.

"Now!" Underhill's voice was ice cold.

The redhead's hands slumped to her side. She looked around for support. There was none. Her entire body deflated. She scooped up her clothes and exited the room.

Underhill pointed to Lydia, the buxom blonde standing beside Nara. "You go with Johnny." This wasn't fair and Lydia was about to tell Underhill so. But the door clicking behind the woman who'd dared protest Underhill's latest edict changed Lydia's mind; she smiled and shuffled over to Johnny.

Lydia reached for Johnny's gonads. "I hope I didn't hurt you too much?"

He blocked her hand but she managed to pinch his nipple. Johnny grabbed her hand, twisted it and used his other hand to twist Lydia's nipple. "When we get back to my room, it'll be my turn."

"I can't wait."

Johnny twisted more. Lydia shut her eyes and smiled.

Angie held tightly on my arm. "Maybe here's hope for me yet..." I'd rather she thought of me as a lover, not as an older brother, but while Underhill and the other two men frolicked in their rooms, maybe I could work on that. And on pumping her for information on Underhill.

The three men retreated to their several rooms. Angie and I followed to make sure everything was okay. Then we went down to the beach for a stroll. We walked close together, enjoying the salt-air breeze. Parts of the beach were lit, some were in darkness. Sometimes our hands brushed against each other, however Angie made no effort to hold hands and I judged it unsafe to attempt that move.

But I had no choice but to attempt to wheedle information out of her. I led her down to the dock and we sat on the cement bench. Small crabs scurried into the inky blackness. "Bernie just wants me to do security," I said. "Are there other things I should be doing for him?"

"He'll let you know if there are."

"What type of things does he get you to do for him?"

"Sometimes miscellaneous errands. But mostly travel arrangements."

"You have your own computer?"

"No, I use Joel's. It's the only computer Bernie uses."

Every fibre of my being cried out for me to push Angie for more details. She had access to Underhill's itinerary for the past *two* years! Not to mention, access to the all-important computer. But my instincts told me that any further questions would be reported straight back to Underhill.

Instead, I pointed to the moon shimmering on the water. "Isn't that beautiful?"

She nodded and leaned against me. Our hands pressed together. I touched my fingers to the inside of hers, but she didn't reciprocate. This was worse than high school!

After a stroll and a snack at the beach grill, I escorted Angie to her room. Not even a peck on my lips.

Back in my own room, I took stock of my investigation. So far, the only thing solid that I had to work on was obtaining corroboration of the payment made to the Jamaican politician. And since I was the one who'd made the payment, there was an obvious entrapment defence. Not exactly solid.

So, after two months of hard work, all I'd accomplished was to insert myself into the distant periphery of Underhill's operation. My gut continued to tell me that I was right about Underhill being involved in human trafficking, likely of the most vile variety. But gut feelings, no matter how strong, would not earn me reinstatement. Nor would they garner the attention of a prosecuting Crown Attorney, Jamaican *or* Canadian.

I sighed as I activated the bare-bones cellphone I'd stashed under a false bottom in the safe inside the closet. If the false bottom were discovered, it would appear to be a writing pad left behind by a previous guest, as would the cellphone. I uploaded the latest installment of my novel from my laptop into the cellphone and added explicit references to Underhill and his operation, including today's events. This version I uploaded to the internet 'cloud'. Then I wiped the cellphone clean of these transactions.

I wished, not for the first time, that I had the resources to perform background checks on Underhill's women, especially Angie and Jacqueline Warne, the newcomer. Background checks were usually a goldmine of information which could be used to turn a target into a viable asset. I didn't know enough about Angie to accomplish this. Worse, beyond her vapid social media accounts, I knew absolutely squat about Jacqueline Warne.

With these unhappy thoughts bouncing around my head, I drifted off to sleep.

Chapter 3 *Jackie*

The next day, I woke up tired and stiff. This was a little from being cramped in a plane for several hours but mostly from the carnal contortions I'd been through with Bernie the night before. Today would be a rest day. Seeking out Underhill again too soon might scare him off.

So, first I'd file my report, then it would be off to the spa for a relaxing massage followed by a mani-pedi. Since I might have to video conference with my boss, I threw off my pajamas, replacing them with bra, panties, T-shirt and jeans.

The beginning of my report, the mundane travel and arrival confirmations were easy enough. So were my descriptions of Underhill's crew, since only Kyle Fairbairn was unknown to the Bureau. His hair was short, greying. But his eyebrows were still dark and he carried himself with a relaxed virility. His moustache was salt and pepper. He had several tattoos: A dragon on his left shoulder, New Zealand tribal on his right. He had a long scar in the center of his lower abdomen which took a curious detour around his navel.

Describing my encounter with Underhill was more difficult.

I stared at my computer screen, uncertain where to begin. The first thing I had to do was to sort out my feelings for Underhill. If I couldn't figure out how to control my emotions and conceal my intentions from him, this would be the shortest undercover assignment in F.B.I. history.

I took a deep breath and shut my eyes. Having sex with a target was a clear violation of Bureau policy. First it put me at risk. Second it would taint any testimony I might give—everything I wanted to prove would now have to be independently corroborated. And third, sex would open me up to emotional manipulation, even compromise. The bottom line was that it might even lead to the termination of my Special Agent status.

I took another deep breath and opened my eyes. Part of my brain registered the computer sitting on the dresser in front of me and the room behind me in the mirror. But my core consciousness was moving through a disciplined martial arts routine. This was my karate black-belt kata, the stylized combat routine I'd physically executed hundreds of times and at least as many more in my head. Today, as for many of the previous repetitions, I was using it as an anchor. Today as I blocked and parried imaginary blows, I etched it into my mind. Today as my body spun and whirled, I created a fortress into which no one would ever infiltrate.

I took another deep breath and began to type. My report was factually accurate, except for a gap that I glossed over. I flirted with Underhill but didn't invite him to my room. After the show we had drinks at the beach bar and engaged in the type of desultory conversation engaged in between adults who will never see each other in the future but who hope to have sex together before the week is out. Pelicans dove into the water.

I described every detail I could recall of Kyle Fairbairn paying-off of the Jamaican politician. I concluded my report with a request for a thorough background check on Underhill's new security chief.

My computer beeped. It was Claire, my roommate, over videophone. She wasn't my *real* roommate. I was still living alone in the vague hope that someday there'd be someone of the opposite sex to welcome into my crazy life. Still, she was the only person in the world that I could tell everything and anything to without fear of judgment. She would know what parts of my report to pass on to our superiors and what to leave out. I felt myself relax as her face came on.

"How was your trip?" she asked.

"Everything fine." This was code for no problems, everything as expected.

"The resort is nice?"

"The best." All my equipment has arrived safe and sound.

"How's the food?"

"Fine so far." This was our code for no problems and that I'd be able to file my report. The 'so far' would allow her to keep repeating the question.

"Meet any special people?"

"A few." I've met my target and inserted myself. Claire knew who to call at the Bureau if I got into trouble, but she wouldn't report any corners I might be cutting.

"You seem tense."

I was suddenly aware that I was playing with my hair and that she'd seen it. I put my hands in my lap and intertwined my fingers. "Just the usual."

"I want you to relax, Jackie." My real name was Jennifer.

She was telling me that I should be Jackie, not Jennifer.

"I *am* relaxed. I met someone."

"What's he like?"

"Tall, dark and muscular!"

"What about his special muscle?" She was asking whether I'd had sex with Underhill.

"*Very* special! I had multiples." We had previously argued about multiple orgasms. Neither of us had experienced the phenomenon. I'd denied their reality, Claire had maintained that they existed.

"Go girl!"

"How're things back home?" I was asking whether there was any scuttlebutt at the F.B.I. But a stranger listening in would hear two girls chatting, not me testing my lifeline.

"I went out on a date, but he wasn't my type." Nothing new.

"Come on, girl, there must—" Suddenly there was a knock on my door. "Sorry, Claire, I have to go, someone's at the door."

She blew me a kiss and then the screen went blue.

When I opened the door, two of Underhill's ladies, the African American, and the east Asian, were standing on the landing. Up close, the black woman's curves, especially her fulsome bosom were even more pronounced. She oozed sexuality. The lithe Asian was equally sensuous, but there was a sharpness to it.

Shaneese, the black woman, smiled at me. "The boss wants us to check you out," she told me in a melodious Jamaican accent.

I waved them into the suite. Nara made a beeline to my computer and proceeded to check out every nook and cranny of my hard drive, even some areas of which I was previously unaware. Shaneese proceeded to empty the contents of every drawer onto the bed and then to inspect each drawer's underside.

Shaneese was wearing a half T-shirt, pink, which covered the top of her chest but left her tummy bare. Every time she bent to check the contents of a drawer, her very skimpy red shorts slid into her butt crack and perfectly cupped her ripe round rump. Thankfully her inspection of my suitcases was not as thorough as her search of my dresser and she missed the false compartment that contained my sidearm and surveillance equipment. Strict protocols meant that I only put the pistol in the bedside drawer at night.

Nara, the east Asian, continued to type away on my laptop. She was dressed in a flowing white diaphanous robe that allowed glimpses of her equally white one-piece swimsuit whenever the two garments touched. My conversation with Claire played back on the screen. How Nara had managed that, I had no idea. Finally, Nara turned the computer off and shut its lid, a disappointed look on her face. Apparently the Bureau had done a good job of hiding my portal to the cloud.

"So, I passed?" I asked, pleased with the subtle undercurrent of sarcasm I'd succeeded in injecting into the question.

"The first test, yes," said Shaneese.

"Mr. Underhill insists that all his girls have maximum flexibility," said Nara.

"Who says I'm one of—"

"Would you like to see Mr. Underhill again?"

"Yes, but—"

"*Maximum* flexibility."

"Okay. Sure."

A glint flashed into Nara's eyes. She pointed to Shaneese. "Touch her."

I touched the black woman's belly. Her skin was as soft as silk. And warm, ever so warm.

"Touch her *sexually*."

I'd never been with a woman, not even in college. I quickly reviewed how I liked being touched. But I sensed that Shaneese would want a more direct approach. I slowly slid my hand up her belly and under her pink half-T. She smiled back at me, white teeth filling her black lips. Her bra was smooth, almost as smooth as her skin. It seemed to take an eternity to climb up her huge mounds, but then I touched something coarser. Two somethings.

I ran my fingers around her areolae, pleased with the shortening of Shaneese's breathing. "Go, girl," she whispered. I suddenly remembered that she had heard my conversation with Claire when Nara had played it back. I pushed my fingers to the center of the black woman's areolae.

Shaneese gasped when I touched her nipples. They were hard little buds. I had expected them to be larger, given their perches atop twin Mount Everests. But there was nothing small about Shaneese's pupils—she was definitely enjoying herself.

"Take off her bra," commanded Nara from behind.

Shaneese turned around and removed her T in one fluid motion. I undid the clasp—four hooks! —of her bra and she turned back facing me as her bra clattered to the floor. My hands regained contact with her breasts, but further down. She grabbed my wrists and pulled my fingers back to her nipples. The buds were larger, warmer. She pulled me backwards until her back touched the wall.

"Touch me lower," breathed Shaneese, spreading her legs, just in case I was in doubt as to her meaning.

I dropped my hands to her hips. The material on her shorts was infused with spandex making her shorts so tight it was as if they were painted on her skin. I could feel her warmth right through them.

"Lower," she breathed, jutting her crotch forward and undoing the button at the top of her zipper.

I touched the zipper with my right hand, keeping my left on her hip.

"Do it girl," she demanded.

I rubbed my finger up and down the front of her zipper.

Shaneese groaned.

"Undo her zipper," said Nara.

I did as I was told. Shaneese wasn't wearing panties. Only a thin fuzz of curls stood between her sex and my fingers.

"Lower," sighed Shaneese.

Whereas the skin on her breasts had been warm, the skin on her vulva was hot. Even this far away, I could smell her sexual aroma, a pungent mix of oysters and jerk chicken.

Behind me, I felt hands lift my T-shirt up and my bra being unclasped. Then both were lifted over my head, breaking my connection with Shaneese. I heard them hit the dresser. Shaneese sighed in protest and I returned my right hand to her vulva, to the heat right next to her pussy. She moaned in appreciation.

Shaneese turned slightly, brushing my fingers across her pussy lips. They were soft and she shuddered. There was a hint of warm dampness. I was vaguely aware of my jeans being undone, more aware of my nudity. I shivered, both from cold and excitement.

"More," breathed Shaneese.

Thin fingers gripped my breasts, one finger above my nipples, one below. "Touch her breasts," directed Nara.

"No!" protested Shaneese. "I want—"

"*This* is what Bernie wants."

Shaneese whimpered as I caressed her nipples and as much

of her breasts as my fingers could reach. Her nipples had grown in size, but her areolae seemed to have shrunk, as if they'd been drawn into the nipples.

"Follow my lead," said Nara her lips less than an inch from my left ear. "Touch her the same way I'm touching you."

Nara gripped my nipples between thumb and forefinger and gave them a slight twist. "I'm going to twist until you yell 'stop'," she whispered in my ear.

I squeezed Shaneese's nipples and twisted. "I'm going to twist until you yell 'stop'," I told her in a clear voice. Her nipples were higher than the width of my finger. She gasped as Nara and I kept twisting.

"Ow!" Shaneese and I yelled in unison. I was pleased that Shanees's 'ow' was louder than mine. But my nipples hurt! I twisted harder, silently begging Shaneese to yell 'stop'.

Nara started to vibrate her fingers. That made my nipples feel *much* better. I tried to imitate what she was doing but since Shaneese showed no reaction, I apparently failed. The black woman kept muttering 'ow'.

Nara twisted again. "Ow!" I yelled as I twisted Shaneese's nipples.

"Stop!" yelled Shaneese. I dropped my arms to my sides and felt Nara grab each of my butt cheeks.

"Touch her down below," whispered Nara. Her breath on my neck sent a tingle down my spine.

Shaneese was even hotter than before and maybe a bit more aroused. Her pussy lips were definitely more swollen, firmer. They barely moved when I touched them.

"Inside," whispered Nara.

One finger slipped right into Shanasee's pussy so I added another and could now feel her gripping both.

"Now, touch your pubic bones together."

"No," whimpered Shaneese as I withdrew my fingers to comply with Nara's latest direction. With only minor adjustments to our legs and knees, we managed to touch pubic bones.

As soon as we'd stopped, Nara slapped my butt. "Now grind."

I wasn't quite sure what to do, but Shaneese knew *exactly* what to do. She reached around, grabbed my butt and ground her pubic prominence into mine, using a clockwise rotating motion.

I gasped.

"Girl, that feels good!" enthused Shaneese.

I snaked my arms through hers and did my best to grab ahold of her butt. Almost all the front of my body was pressed against hers and her movements were caressing up and down—chest, breasts, nipples, tummy and thighs. I started to match her movements and since my clockwise motions were counter to hers, they intensified the sensations we were each giving each other.

Shaneese rocked her hips as she continued her circular grinding. Our clits brushed together. "Girl, that feel's *great!*" she keened.

We had been going at it for a couple of minutes and I was starting to become thoroughly aroused. I wasn't close to a climax, which was okay; orgasms were for sex with men. But this was nice, *very* nice!

Nara was behind me, her body pressed against my back. I could feel her swimsuit. She must have removed her robe. She was matching my movements. With her pressed up against me, I could relax my legs and concentrate on enjoying this feminine sandwich.

Nara began to slide down my back and slide her hands under my butt, holding me even firmer both upright and against Shaneese. Shaneese and I were beginning to sweat which allowed us to slide more freely. And the voluptuous black woman was becoming ever more efficient in targeting my clit. I felt a frisson dance deep inside and I gasped. Surely I wasn't ready to come?!

Nara had now left my back. One hand on my butt was holding me up. The other was caressing my thigh. Little jolts were dancing between Shaneese's pubic bone and Nara's fingers. The jolts intensified the closer her fingers got to Shaneese's sex.

Then Nara's fingers touched the bottom of my sex. I shuddered deep inside.

No! Yes. *No!* I couldn't come with a woman. I was—

Fingers slid inside my pussy. *Feminine* fingers! I could tell by the way that they were sliding in and out that I was completely wet. Maybe that would protect me. I was too wet to really feel anything.

Shaneese's clit did a complete circle around mine and I was floating, only dimly aware that a soft cloth was being pressed inside me, removing excess moisture. Panties? Then Nara's fingers returned inside me. And that, I was *totally* aware of! Every thrust made my pussy squeeze her fingers more firmly.

"Let go," urged Nara from below.

"Let go," echoed Shaneese.

I tried to stop it, to save myself, but the force of the sensations being inflicted on me conspired with the urgings inside my sex and I felt the first twinge. I struggled to suppress the second twinge, but that just made it all the stronger.

"No!" I screamed.

"Yes," whispered Nara from below as she added a counterclockwise rotation to her thrusts.

The third twinge was unmistakable and it overwhelmed my resistance. The fourth twinge was a hard contraction. "Shit!" I screamed. Then contraction after contraction after *contraction*. My whole body was warm waves of pleasure with jolt after jolt of delight in my pussy.

As my orgasm faded, I felt myself being carried onto the bed where two pairs of hands laid me gently on my back.

"Now it's our turn," Nara told me.

Before I understood what she was saying, I felt the bed jiggle beneath my head as Shaneese's knees positioned themselves beside my ears. Then her sex lowered to just above my face. I reached my left hand up to play with her pubic curls. The fingers of my right hand fluttered up and down her pussy lips. The delicate pink labia were hot and engorged but, given their length, still flexible. Above me, Shaneese moaned.

I lifted my head and managed to run my tongue along the lower edge of her pussy lips. She trembled and moaned again. Up close, her pungent mix of oysters and jerk chicken assailed my nose.

Shaneese slowly lowered herself as I flicked my tongue up and down the leading edge of her pussy lips. The back of my head flattened down on the mattress but Shaneese kept coming lower. Her bum rested lightly on my chest, pinning me to the bed. I was licking down the entire sides of Shaneese's pussy lips, right to where flimsy flutters connected with plump heat. She quivered every time I circled around her clit. Her breaths were moans.

Nara was dancing her fingers up and down my body. She ran her fingers through my pubic hair and lightly caressed my breasts. But she avoided my pussy and nipples.

Shaneese adjusted her thighs and my tongue stumbled between her pussy lips. The first taste of her jerk spice stung my tongue, but oysters soothed the sting away. Her juices flowed freely and I had to swallow again and again to avoid being suffocated. She ground her sex into my face, grunting and groaning, louder with each rotation.

Then she went completely still. Her thighs tensed hard against my ears. Her whole body shuddered, shaking the bed so violently I thought it might fall apart. My tongue licked up and down as fast as it could, but her weight made this difficult. I felt Nara straddling my body, helping Shaneese to hold herself upright.

"Jesus!" screamed Shaneese.

The bed continued to shake. Shaneese's screams were loud, but now incomprehensible. I struggled to breathe as her whole weight pressed down onto my face. Finally her shudders began to dissipate. She slid off and collapsed beside me, her head by my thighs.

I heaved air into my lungs. Nara looked down at me. She was entirely nude. Her body was like a willow in spring, two dark buds on her breasts ready to flower forth. Her shoulder-length black hair shimmered in the breeze. Beside me, Shaneese was snoring softly.

When Nara was satisfied that I'd recovered from my bout with Shaneese, she pulled me sideways, away from the big black woman, and climbed on top of me. Unlike Shaneese, she faced down toward my hips, her butt just over my forehead. I caught a whiff of sushi and soy sauce.

Nara's pussy lips were barely visible, two elegant pink strands at the center of her sex. "Are you ready?" she asked. "Shaneese was already half way to heaven when she climbed atop you."

I suddenly remembered my fingers on the black woman's pussy and Nara behind me. The Asian woman was starting cold. I took a deep breath. "Ready."

"Pull a pillow under your head."

I did and she flopped forward to all fours. Her pussy was almost a foot above my face. I reached out and stroked lightly up and down her elegant little lips. She began to purr. She had a tuft of dark black pubic hair. I anchored my left hand with the black curls and pulled up, stretching her pussy lips and bringing her clit into view. Every time I stroked up and down her pussy lips, I came closer and closer to her clit.

The first time I touched her clit, Nara's whole body shuddered. The second time, her torso stiffened, holding her motionless. As I moved my fingers lower, she groaned, "Time for your tongue."

I pulled my hands away as she angled her sex back and down towards my face. She trembled just before contact. Had she felt my breath? I flicked my tongue up and down her pussy lips, causing her hips to quiver. Slow strokes of my tongue up and down her pussy held her motionless. Pushing it inside caused her to gasp for air.

"Faster!" demanded Nara.

I lapped up and down her pussy as fast as I could. She moaned, gradually louder. And her pussy was saltier. But otherwise she held herself still. My neck was starting to stiffen when she began to slowly rock her hips forward, effectively increasing the speed of my strokes.

I remembered a lover who'd given particularly good head and started to shake my head slowly back and forth. This and her rocking motion, caused my tongue to rub across her pussy lips and half circle around her clit, sometimes from the top, sometimes from the bottom. Nara's body began to shake. The shakes were soft and subtle, but they ran up and down the length of her body.

"Harder!" she gasped.

I rolled her over onto her back. This roused Shaneese and I felt her get off the bed. But my focus was on Nara. I slid two fingers into her pussy and tickled her anus with another. While I was sliding my fingers in and out, I used my other hand to pull her skin away from her clit which I began to lightly suck.

Nara dug her fingers into my calves. "Harder!"

I slid another finger inside her and pressed harder with the one on her back door. It too began to slide inside. Nara groaned appreciatively. I sucked on her clit as hard as I dared.

"Harder!" she demanded.

But instead of harder, I went faster.

"Harder," she screamed. Faster I went.

Then there was a contraction, unmistakable on my fingers, then another. I jabbed my fingers into her as far as they would go, then made short twirling thrusts. My mouth sucked on her clit as hard as it could.

"Fuck!" she screamed. Hard contractions around my fingers. She bucked. My hands flew off. Only my mouth maintained contact. I grabbed her butt. She bucked again, her whole body wracked by contractions. "Aiee!" I did my best to suck and wiggle my tongue across her entire sex but her contractions sent it sliding this way and that.

"Fuck!" screamed Nara. Nonetheless, her contractions were weakening.

"Fuck," she gasped, then moaned, her arms flopping to the bed, her body completely still. I sucked and stroked her sex until she stopped groaning.

When I lifted myself up, Shaneese was looking on, admiration in her eyes. Nara propped herself up on her elbows.

"Wow! That was spectacular!" I told them.

"That was your first time, wasn't it?" asked Shaneese.

I nodded.

"Then we have to make it memorable."

"It's already been memorable."

I started to get off the bed. But Shaneese shook her head. "We're not finished yet." Nara looked at her quizzically. Shaneese pointed at my crotch. "I want to taste her twat."

Nara shrugged. I was already half off the bed, but Shaneese knelt down, her body below mine and pulled my pussy onto her face. Nara helped me to steady myself and position my thighs beneath the outer edges of two black, and very warm, breasts.

Shaneese's tongue thrust into my insides. Three wiggling strokes and I was in the thrall of carnality. Three more wiggling strokes sent jolts up into my lungs, forcing me to gasp for air. Nara sidled up beside Shaneese and kissed me, her tongue darting deep into my mouth. Two tongues ignited fire up and down my body.

Nara broke off the kiss. I tried to breathe, but Shaneese's tongue was still working its mischief down below. Nara looked deep into my eyes and my entire body, my entire soul, melted. She positioned her pointing finger against her thumb, readying to flick her finger. Part of me had no idea what she was doing. Part of me knew *exactly* what she was about to do.

"Ready?" asked Nara.

Shaneese grunted below, but didn't flag in her exertions. Somehow her grunts moved me further into the maw of the impending orgasm. I shook my head but gasped as Shaneese hit a particularly sensitive spot.

"Ready?" repeated Nara.

I was ready, but I shook my head.

Somehow the Asian woman detected my fib. "Shut your eyes," she said and the force of her words drew my eyelids down.

As soon as there was darkness, I felt a stinging on my nipples. My eyes rocketed open. The stinging was centered on my barbells. Nara's fingers were cocked behind her thumbs, ready for another attack. "Shut your eyes," she demanded.

This time I shut my eyes of my own accord, steeling myself for another attack on my barbells. But the attack came from below—Shaneese nipped my clit.

"Ow!" I protested.

Her tongue immediately soothed the hurt and pushed me to the cusp of climax.

"Let go," demanded Nara.

"No!" I shook my head.

Her lips brushed mine. "Let go," she breathed.

I held on, teetering on the cusp, everything above Shaneese's tongue hot and wet, wrenched so tight my hips hurt.

"Let go," breathed Nara, igniting a spark inside my throat. Boom! Everything below let go in a massive explosion of pleasure. Two searing jolts on my nipples. The pleasure rocketed up my spine sending me flying into white-hot ecstasy. Spasm after spasm whipped up my spine.

Wave after wave of delight lapped against my body, the two women on either side of me sharing in the transcendent moment.

Afterwards, when we returned to the terrestrial here and now, Nara looked at me seriously. "Bernie likes you."

"How do you know?" I asked.

"Because he never bothers to check most women out," Shaneese said from below as she rose to sit beside me. "He doesn't keep them around long enough to make it worth the bother."

"What about you two?"

"He made me stand on one foot while he interrogated me," said Shaneese.

I raised my eyes in Nara's direction.

"He made me box Mr. Ritchie."

She mimed a one-two jab, then a vicious uppercut. I felt deep pity for Joel.

Nara looked at her watch. Suddenly she and Shaneese stood and dressed. We exchanged kisses and they left.

After I made sure that the door was securely shut behind them, that they hadn't left anything behind, I pulled out my laptop and reinitialized its electronic countermeasures. Half an hour later the report of my encounter with Shaneese and Nara was ready. I did a quick scan to ensure that the omission of the sexual aspects of the encounter was not noticeable. Then I pressed [send] and it was in the cloud and likely being poured over by the team back at F.B.I. headquarters.

Now I definitely deserved a reward! I dragged myself to the spa, each step acquainting me with muscles and ligaments of which I'd previously been unaware.

The masseur was a young east Indian chap. Very skilled. After only ten minutes, he had turned my muscles to jelly and I had to fight to keep awake.

I described Underhill and his entourage. "Have they been to the spa?" I asked.

"Uh hmmm."

"Good tippers?"

"So sorry, we are not allowed to take tips."

"So I've heard. But did they leave anything under the towels when they left?"

"Pretty lady, please."

I hardened my voice. "Did they leave anything?"

"Mr. Underhill, yes. Mr. Ritchie and the ladies, no." That made sense, Underhill was a narcissistic extrovert. Ritchie and the women were just along for the ride. But it also meant that they were stingy and possibly open to financial incentives.

"Did they ever talk about business?"

"No, lady, never!" There was fear in his voice which meant that someone had. The fear also meant that trying to pry it out of him might expose my cover. I made a mental note to install a listening device before I left.

Towards the end of the massage he started dropping hints about a happy ending. I brushed his hints firmly aside. I'd had too many happy endings already for one day. Then I immediately regretted my decision. A happy ending from the masseur would have reset my heterosexuality…

The mani-pedi was heavenly, especially since it was at Bureau expense. Only Nara had come in to have her nails done. The esthetician was afraid of her and I was pretty sure that Nara hadn't confided in the staff. The esthetician gratefully accepted a tip, something that might get her fired from the resort.

As I was about to leave, I ran into a young Jamaican who was cleaning the rooms. "I heard you asking about Mr. Underhill," he told me.

I nodded.

He cleared his throat and wobbled from one foot to the other. I made a show of inserting a twenty-dollar bill inside a towel and tossing it into the soiled linen bin. His face immediately brightened. "Mr. Underhill asked, 'Cas pack on tarnitood' and Mr. Ritchie responded 'Jah. See on ohutult vaorgus'."

I hurried back towards my room. Blue sky, breezes, and happy couples failed to distract me from trying to guess what my masseuse could have told me.

Once I'd booted up my computer, I did my best to enter what the young Jamaican janitor had told me into Google Translate. After almost an hour, it turned out that Underhill and Ritchie were speaking Estonian.

Underhill had asked, "Was the package delivered?" Ritchie had responded, "Yes. It's safely in the network."

'Package' could mean anything from thumbtacks to a thermonuclear device. Or a container-load of human beings.

Chapter 4 *Kyle*

I watched nonchalantly as Johnny did his customary morning security sweep around the tables which Underhill had staked out as his own. Ostensibly, I was supervising his efforts, but there really wasn't much to it. All he had to do was run a wand over everything and wave me over if it beeped.

As soon as Johnny finished, I made a show of inspecting one of the columns supporting the open-air dining room. But what I was really doing was planting a small camera pointed at the spot where I'd guessed Joel would open Underhill's laptop. So far I'd guessed wrong with my daily placements, but sooner or later the odds would move in my favor and I'd have a recording of what Underhill and Ritchie were up to.

Half an hour of boredom later, punctuated by watching semi-clad women and eating a steaming ham and cheese omelette—a man could only eat so much pineapple—Joel turned up.

He opened the laptop right in the center of the camera's field of view. I almost choked to death swallowing my chortles of glee. Now, all I had to do was go to my room, activate the camera, and start recording.

From what I'd gathered yesterday, something big was in the works. Underhill had repeatedly asked about "the shipment". After extensive keyboarding sessions, Joel had looked up from his computer. He'd had Underhill's full attention. "Package confirmed," Joel had said.

"All the arrangements?"

Joel had nodded, "Multiple packages requiring individual attention, some large, some medium and especially the valuable small ones."

If I could activate my little camera and record Joel and Underhill completing their transaction, this part of their vile network would be brought down for good.

I took a deep breath to calm my nerves. "Joel, I have to—" But a large swarthy hand on my shoulder cut short my excuse to go to my room. Underhill had snuck up behind me without my even noticing! I turned around, readying an excuse as to why I hadn't seen him approaching.

Thankfully Underhill had other things on his mind. "Kyle. I want you to help Jackie deliver a packet to Sangster." He lifted a brown packet held together with brown tape, the prototypical kilo of cocaine. Sangster International was Montego Bay's airport.

Jackie was strolling along a distant path and he waved for her to come over. She had obviously gotten into the Irie-vibe of Hedo; her bikini top was two skimpy white triangles, her bikini bottom a knitted mesh which revealed hints of the snout of her salamander tattoo.

As she approached, Underhill turned to me. "You'll be there to protect Jackie, and the package, in case the local pot heads try to rip her off. But in the distance. Just in case." That meant that I'd be far enough in the background and wouldn't be arrested if the police found the drugs.

Jackie came up and Underhill kissed her on the lips. She reciprocated, and then some. When they came up for air, he pecked her on the cheek and pointed to me. "I want you to run an errand for me. Kyle will go with you to keep you safe." He lifted out the kilo-size package he'd just shown me. "I need you to deliver this to my customs broker in Montego Bay. Can you do this for me?"

She took the package and held it gingerly. "What's in it?"

"It's a sample of an exotic type of sea salt. Special healing properties."

Jackie looked at the package. Anyone who'd watched the news or more than two movies would know that the packet contained drugs, likely cocaine, and a lot of it. "Shouldn't it have an envelope?" she asked.

Underhill snapped his fingers, not taking his eyes of Jackie as Joel handed her a pre-addressed bubble-wrap envelope. "Right you are my dear."

Jackie hesitated a moment, then carefully placed the kilo packet inside the envelope and sealed it. She tested the seal, then plopped it into her shoulder bag. She made a lascivious motion with her hips. "Sure, baby. For you, anything." 'Anything' was drawn out in an exaggeratedly seductive fashion which both she and Underhill found hilarious.

Jackie started to sway her hips towards the buffet but Underhill's voice stopped her in her tracks. "Kyle will go with you."

She turned around and looked me up and down. I did my best to act nonchalant. She shrugged and turned back towards the buffet. But this time she walked naturally, no exaggerated sway to her hips.

After breakfast, we changed clothes and took a small minibus into Mo Bay. It was run by one of the large travel companies and thus wouldn't attract any attention from the authorities. Jackie sat up front, chatting up the driver. I sat in the back, but on the aisle so that I could maintain line of sight on her.

Underhill's customs broker's "office" was a short counter in the airport's customs hall. Other brokers also had counters. Most of them had a line-up of customers waiting to be served, but not Underhill's.

Jackie made a beeline to Underhill's custom broker. She didn't look left, she didn't look right. Was she really that naïve? So nervous she wasn't thinking? Or just trying to act innocent? I lingered at the far end of the customs hall, doing my best to look inconspicuous by chatting up another clerk with an inquiry about shipping a barrel to Toronto.

Jackie reached into her purse and carefully placed the package on the counter in front of Underhill's custom's broker. He angled his head around to see the address on the package. Why didn't he just turn—

Two disheveled men jumped out of the line leading to the broker next to Underhill's. They grabbed Jackie's arms. I took a step towards them but another customer, this one in a suit, thrust a badge in Jackie's face. "Jamaica Constabulary," he announced.

At the mention of 'Constabulary', the customs hall swiftly emptied. The man in the suit looked at the package on the counter. He was tall and skinny with a face composed of harsh angles. His suit was white linen, his hands and face a shiny ebony; his eyes were a microcosm of the rest of him. His nose was as long as the beak of a crane and about to spear Jackie's package as if it were a fish. Jackie continued to struggle. I tried to melt into the wall.

The suit turned to Jackie and held up his hand. "My name is Inspector Morant. I am with the Jamaica Constabulary Force's Narcotics Division." Something in his look made her stop struggling.

Morant held his hand out towards Underhill's custom's clerk. In a flash there was a box-cutting knife in his hand. Morant made a surgical slice across the top of the envelope and pulled out the packet wrapped in brown tape. "What do we have here?" he asked the packet. His accent was impeccably British.

No one answered.

Morant lifted up the packet, his shirt poking an inch out from the sleeve of his jacket, and turned to Jackie. "What do we have here?" he repeated.

Jackie tried to shake herself free, but the grip of the men holding her arms remained solid. "I don't know," she said.

"I don't know," mimicked Morant, lapsing into a deep Jamaican lilt. Then he nodded to one of the men holding Jackie. "Take her to the station."

It was time for me to find the men's room and call Underhill to report.

As they turned Jackie towards the door, she spotted me and angled her head in my direction. "I'm with him," she yelled.

I froze in my tracks.

"Bring him too," said Morant, once more reverting to his British accent.

I did a quick calculation of the distance to the door. Morant's cops were closer. I stood still and raised my hands.

They took us to the police station in separate squad cars. Morant went with Jackie. The guy driving me was more interested in listening to loud Reggae music than interrogating. That suited me fine.

Almost as soon as my handcuffs had been removed and I'd been sat down in a small room with cinder block walls and a metal table, the very sturdy door creaked on its hinges. Morant sat down opposite me. He smiled. "She says she got the drugs from you."

"I doubt that very much," I told him. I didn't know if I had the right to ask for a lawyer, but I didn't need legal advice to tell me that I shouldn't volunteer any information.

Morant shrugged and stood. "Why don't you come see for yourself?" He ushered me into another room, even smaller than the one we'd just exited. Same sturdy door, same cinder-block walls, same peeling paint. But no table and this one had a large window on one side. I recognized it as a one-way mirror.

In the room opposite the window, Jackie was being frisked by two female Jamaican cops. The thin one threw Jackie's tee shirt onto the table and picked up her shorts. The rotund one squeezed Jackie's breasts, then bent down to inspect the center of her bra. "What we have here?" she asked.

"What you see?" asked her partner.

"Sometin' strange."

"Careful now," said the thin one as she unclasped Jackie's bra.

The rotund cop slowly pulled Jackie's bra off, holding it as if it might explode. She carefully placed it on top of the tee shirt and angled her head sideways to inspect Jackie's nipple stud. "What dat?"

"It's a nipple barbell," said Jackie, feigning boredom.

"It hurt?"

"Not now."

The rotund cop reached out and touched the stud.

"Is that necessary?" asked Jackie.

The rotund cop shrugged. "Spread your legs."

Jackie complied. When the rotund cop pressed her hand into the centre of Jackie's genitals, she lifted Jackie's heels off the floor. Jackie's face showed extreme discomfort, but she kept her mouth shut. I was momentarily proud of her.

Then the two cops bent Jackie over the side of the table and looked at her bum. Her bum was facing away from us, so I couldn't see what they were doing. But from the look on Jackie's face, I could guess.

The two female cops sat Jackie down on the opposite side of the table. They left through the creaking door. Jackie put her bra back on and wiggled her panties back into place.

"Showtime!" said Morant and left the room.

Jackie looked over at her tee shirt and shorts, as if wondering whether to put them back on. But before she could decide, Morant entered the room, sat down opposite her and made a show of turning on a tape recorder.

"Miss Warne," he said, "tell me again, for the record, what you told me in the squad car on the way to the station."

"I received the package from Kyle, the man you arrested, early this morning. He said it was a simple matter of dropping it off at customs and then he'd take me on a tour of Montego Bay."

"What is Kyle's last name?"

"I know him only as Kyle. We met last night." There was something professional, practiced about the way she was telling her story, but I was too focused on what she was saying to worry about it.

"Why did you agree to deliver the packet?"

"He was a friend. It was no big deal."

"You said you only met him last night."

"It was a very memorable night."

"Memorable how?"

"Memorable as in it's private."

"Private enough for you to spend the next ten years in a Jamaican jail if you don't tell me?"

"He was good in bed. *Very* good in bed."

Morant pressed the 'OFF' button on his tape recorder. "Why don't you tell me the details and then we can decide what we need to put on the record."

"Why don't you test what's in the packet?" She took a deep breath, pressing the outline of her nipple pin into her bra.

"All in good time, Miss Warne. Now please, the details of your encounter with 'Kyle'."

She sighed, making an exaggerated show of her exhalation. "He's big and stocky, you saw that. But on the dance floor, he was smooth, guiding me around as if I was floating on air. Then the music slowed and he brought me closer, not touching, but close enough I could feel his warmth and smell his musk." She groaned.

Morant adjusted himself in his seat, then motioned for her to continue.

"I was the one who took the next step, allowing our chests to touch. His heat penetrated right through my nipple pin." She touched it, wiggling its outline under the thin material of her bra. "By the end of the song, his cock was hard and pressing against me. Then the music sped up and we danced apart. But this time he wasn't as quick on his feet."

"And then?"

"And then we were both thirsty and we went out to the bar to have a drink."

"That's hardly *private*, Miss Warne."

"Over the drinks, Kyle told me about all the women he'd been with that week. One had wanted to dribble champagne over his cock, then lick it off. Nancy had wanted to be spanked. Patricia had wanted him to suck her privates until he'd swallowed *all* her juices. Georgia had convinced him to explore her back door. Kim wanted him to tie her up, attach a vibrator to her *privates* and talk dirty to her. Jolene—"

"What did the two of *you* do?"

Jackie shrugged and adjusted her breasts. Her nipples were

engorged and had lifted her nipple pins off her skin. Morant shifted in his chair as Jackie took a deep breath.

"Well, we went to his room and we took off our clothes. Did you need the details of that?"

Morant shook his head. His bum squirmed on his chair.

Jackie threw her long black hair back, making sure he got a good look at her breasts. "We laid on the bed. I was on the bottom. Missionary style. But missionary style at Hedo is different. There's a mirror in the ceiling and I could see every muscle on Kyle's butt and he pumped his cock into me. Having sex is always wonderful, but being able to watch a cock plunging into yourself is *special*."

"So, you had sex with Kyle, then what did—"

"Oh, that wasn't the end of it. Then he turned me on top of him and I could see him looking at my butt as he pressed his hips upwards. It was really hot! I relaxed every time it was his turn to press upwards and angled myself towards him. I squeezed his cock as he withdrew and I angled myself away from him. Over and over he plunged himself *all* the way in. Each thrust brushed him against my cli-tor-is. Then I began to squeeze as he pushed upwards, making him work harder, making him look into my eyes. 'You're being a bad girl' he told me. 'I am', I responded. 'Maybe we should both watch', he said.

"Okay, you had sex—"

"Then he pulled himself out of me and laid my back against his stomach. We reinserted his cock inside me and I could see it sliding in and out of my pussy. I have this tattoo." Jackie stood so that Morant could see the hind legs and torso of the amphibian tattoo on her stomach. She pointed to where its head disappeared under her panties. "And every time he slid himself out, it looked as if my salamander was licking my pussy lips."

I felt my face flush.

Morant reached towards his tape recorder, but a quick shake of her head caused him to withdraw his finger.

"Then he dragged me to the side of the bed and put his cock by my mouth. I licked its tip and he inserted a finger into my pussy. I arched my head back sucked his cock into my throat. I couldn't move much, but he rocked his hips and synced his hip movements with the movements of his fingers. I'd never felt so *together* before in my life."

Morant squirmed and reached for his tape recorder, but a

sharp look from Jackie froze his hand in mid-air. I began to wonder whether I should be taking notes.

She took a deep breath and Morant returned his hand to his lap. "I told him that I wanted what Patricia had. Kyle spun me around on the bed so that my legs were dangling over the sides. He laved his tongue up and down my pussy, lapping up her juices. But she produced more and more honeysuckle. He licked and licked. It was too much, but I couldn't escape. Finally his tongue became rough and I realized that his mouth was dry and that so was my pussy. That's when—"

Morant's hand darted out and he stabbed the 'ON' button of his tape recorder. "In short, you had sex with 'Kyle'.

"In *short*, yes." Jackie looked disappointed that her recitation had been prematurely terminated.

"You realize that you're in a lot of trouble," said Morant, trying to look stern.

"I'm not in anything until you test the contents of the packet you seized." I smiled. It's exactly what I would have said.

"Please, Ms. Warne. We all know what is in the package you were delivering to customs."

"Kyle told me that it was exotic sea salt. Is that a crime in Jamaica?"

"No, but coca salt is. Does this 'Kyle' have a last name?"

"I'm sure he does."

"And it is…..?"

"You arrested him, why don't *you* ask him?"

"Why don't you tell me?"

"Why don't you test the contents of the packet?"

"Where did 'Kyle' get the packet?"

"I don't know. Why don't you ask him?"

"I'm asking you."

"I can see that."

"Where did 'Kyle' get the packet?"

"Where are your test results?"

Morant got up and exited the room. His hands were clenched in fists. Jackie looked around the room, then put her shirt and shorts back on.

After a few minutes, Morant came back. He placed a letter-sized envelope on the table between himself and Jackie. "Do you know what this is?"

"My release papers?"

Morant tapped the envelope. "These are the test results you've been nagging about. The ones which will show what is in the packet you were trying to ship out of the country. Do you know what will happen when I open it?"

"You're going to let me go?"

"Miss Warne, you know that's not going to happen. The results will show cocaine. If I open the envelope, I will be unable to offer you any consideration. You will do a minimum of ten years hard time in a Jamaican jail. Trust me when I tell you that our jails are nothing like our resorts. So, you have one last chance to tell me everything you know."

Jackie smiled. "After Kyle's mouth went dry—"

"Not about the lovemaking. About the cocaine."

She shrugged. "I *have* told you everything."

Morant made a show of opening the envelope with excruciating and methodical deliberation. Jackie feigned indifference. Morant leisurely pulled the single sheet of paper out of the envelope, making sure to turn it face down on the steel tabletop. Two fingers and two thumbs gripped the closest corners of the paper. "Last chance, Ms. Warne."

She looked back at him with disdain. Attagirl!

Morant turned the paper over and began to read. It was too far away for me to see, even with my nose pressed against the glass. He scowled, but continued to read. Suddenly he slammed the paper down on the table. "It's salt!" he bellowed, rattling the glass. "Ordinary *table* salt!"

Jackie looked surprised. Momentarily disappointed. She slammed her palm onto the table, at least as hard as Morant had. I was glad I'd removed my nose from the glass. "The bastard!" she shouted. "He told me it was *exotic*, health-food shit! When I get ahold of—"

"You'll have your opportunity soon enough."

Morant led her by the hand, right into the room where I'd been watching. Jackie rushed right at me, pounding her fists on my chest. She was hitting hard, but hitting like a girl. Somehow I had the sense that she could do worse if she really wanted to.

Morant let her beat on me for several minutes. Then he clapped his hands. "That's enough! Take it outside! You're free to go. Both of you!"

On the curb, Jackie placed her hands on her hips and glared at me. The top of the now-opened bubble-wrap envelope containing the now-opened packet of salt was poking out of the top of her shoulder bag. "Bernie's paying for us to go back to the resort with a rental car, isn't he?"

The look on her face told me that there was only one answer she'd accept.

Half an hour later, she strutted down the aisle, chose the most expensive car, got in and slammed the door shut behind her. I held up the keys to the less expensive car I'd chosen, pointed to it, and rapped on the window. Jackie stared straight ahead. I sighed and returned to the rental office. It was a new clerk. He wanted to know exactly where in Negril we would be taking the car.

Twenty minutes later we drove out of the lot in the car *she'd* chosen. Jackie was still staring straight ahead. It began to rain as I negotiated the side streets towards the highway out of the city.

As soon as we turned onto the road leading back to Negril, Jackie banged her fist against the car door. "That had better be the last test *Bernie* has in store for me!"

"You'll have to take that up with Mr. Underhill."

"You're *Mr. Underhill's* head of security. I'm taking it up with you."

I decided that silence was the best policy. She kicked the underside of the dashboard and sulked.

Half an hour later, the sun burst out of the clouds. A beam of sunlight hit her face and Jackie's mood seemed to magically brighten. "How did you like the way I handled the cops?" she asked.

"You mean other than pointing to me at the customs hall?"

"You got what you deserved. Morant was an ass."

"Why did you tell him we were lovers?"

"Because of the way you look at me, all that lust in your eyes!"

"I do not!"

"You do too."

"Mr. Underhill—"

"Does not own your heart."

"We never—"

"But you *wanted* to."

No more than I'd wanted to with any of the other women strutting around Hedo. "I certainly never described the fantasies you told Morant about."

"No?"

"No."

"But aren't the fantasies I described exactly what you think about when you're lying alone in the dark?"

"I've never licked a woman with a dry tongue." Damn! She's going to think that I'm agreeing with all the other outrageous stories she'd told about me.

"But now you're thinking about it, aren't you? What it would feel like to lick up and down my sex with a dry tongue?"

"Wouldn't it hurt?"

"First you'd have to get me really, really turned on. Then the dryness would push me over the edge. Why don't you find a secluded spot? We could give it a try."

I concentrated on maneuvering around a slow-moving delivery lorry. "I don't think that would be wise."

"Don't you want to know what I taste like? How I'll react to your tongue? Whether I'll quiver like a leaf? Or shudder and scream like a hurricane? What will the last drop of juice coming out of my pussy taste like? Will you ever get your finger out? What will a *dry* orgasm really be like?"

"Some things should remain a fantasy." I was going to have a hard time getting to sleep tonight...

"Afraid Mr. Underhill would disapprove?"

"Aren't you?"

"After today's escapade, Mr. Underhill *owes* me."

"Owes you?"

"I've passed test after test. Now he *owes* me."

"Owes you how?"

"He owes me dessert."

"Food is free at Hedonism." Ahead a car was coming straight at me. I readied to hit the ditch in case it didn't return to its lane in time.

"Will the waiters smear chocolate pudding all over my body? Is that part of the all-inclusive package?"

"Probably not." But there was one ebony beauty I'd like to have—

"Then that's what Bernie owes me."

"To make a mess of you?"

"To run his hands all over my body massaging the cool

concoction into every curve and crevice, to slip his fingers—"

"Miss Warne!"

"Mr. Fairbairn!"

"I don't think this is appropriate conversation—"

"Did you turn the mic off during my interrogation?"

I kept my eyes on the road. "Food is for eating," I told her.

"Did you turn the mic off during my interrogation?" I kept my eyes on the road and pretended to have difficulty negotiating a curve. "Or did you listen to every syl-la-ble?"

I felt her turn in her seat, her tongue inches from my ear. "I thought not," she breathed. "I bet you got as hard then as you are now. Just like Morant did. Just *thinking* about it."

"I am not—"

"Hard? Shall we find out? Should I put my hand on your crotch?"

I fought not to squirm in my seat. I was definitely tumescent, but I'd be fine if I could untangle the bent erection inside my pants. "No!" I told her.

"Very well." She settled back into her seat and I exhaled. "But you are going to listen. You're going to get so hard it hurts."

"Please, I—"

"Bernie's going to take the first bowl of chocolate pudding and dip his finger into it. Then he's going to hold his finger just above my lips and let me lick the pudding off it. The pudding is cold and sweet. He'll circle my lips with the next finger full and let me lick it off.

"Then he'll scoop two fingers into the bowl and deposit pudding atop my right nipple followed quickly by a scoop on my left nipple. The pudding's so cold it almost freezes them off. Then his mouth rescues my right nipple and she's warm again. His tongue twirls the last drop of pudding into his mouth. And then he sucks! My right nipple is hard and hot, my left still cold.

"He sucks his lips up to the top of my right nipple, then off. She falls back into my breast. Cold! He's put more pudding on her. Now it's time for my left nipple to feel the heat of his mouth. Round and round my nipple he goes. Hot left, cold right. Then his cock is inside me and I can't tell which nipple is which—all my body is freezing and hot all at the same time."

She favoured me with a smile, as if asking whether she should continue. I shook my head. She shut her eyes and settled back into the seat to take a nap. It took ten minutes for my tumescence to subside. Then I had an hour of silent bliss.

Jackie woke and stretched just as we were entering Negril. I stared straight ahead. Her face clouded and she slumped back into her seat.

She remained slumped in her seat as the palm trees of the resort came into view. She remained slumped in her seat as we drove towards the name of the resort emblazoned in the flower garden by the entrance.

But when Jackie spotted Underhill waiting for us, her face immediately brightened. She sat bolt upright. When I stopped, he opened the door to the car and pulled her into his arms. They hugged and cuddled. Then he gently pried her loose and took her by the hand. "You must be famished," he told her.

It took me almost an hour to negotiate the return of the rental car with the front desk. Then it was time for a shower and change of clothes. By the time I got to the dining room, Underhill was coming up from the beach. Jackie was skipping along next to him, wearing a new dress.

Dinner was a lavish affair with gifts for everyone. I got a pair of sandals, Underhill's way of telling me to loosen up.

After dinner, Underhill took Jackie, and several bowls of pudding, to her room. This left me to listen to general grumblings amongst Underhill's ladies as we ate dessert and watched the show. They were upset with the attention he was lavishing on Jackie, and especially upset with the lack of attention he was paying to them. Joel tried to put his arms around Nara and Shaneese, but they each grabbed an ear and led him away. Johnny and Lydia left holding hands. Only Angie lingered behind.

The camera I'd installed that morning was still up on the column. I ate slowly, hoping that Angie would leave so that I could retrieve the camera. Underhill would have my balls if he discovered it.

But Angie was still there when I returned with dessert. It was time to be proactive. "What do you have planned for the evening?" I asked her.

"I was hoping you'd ask me up to your room." No! What if she wanted to stay the night?! If Johnny found the camera when he did his crack-of-dawn sweep—

I smiled at her. "Or we could go to your room. I'm sure it's nicer."

"The rooms are pretty much the same."

"Yours is probably neater."

She shrugged and smiled. "My room it is."

Inside her room, Angie quickly striped nude. I raced to follow suit. She squatted on the floor, enveloped my penis whole and sucked all the air out of my lungs.

"Whoa girl, slow down!"

She removed her mouth and slouched her back against the bed, her bum on the cold floor. With some difficulty, she let me pull her to her feet.

But she didn't want to look into my eyes. "Sorry," she mumbled.

"Sorry?! What for?"

"For not being a good lover. Bernie doesn't want me. And now neither do you!" She looked as if she was about to break out in tears.

"No, Angie, quite the opposite. That was *fantastic!* I just wanted time to savour how good it was." As soon as the words escaped my lips, I regretted. I should be back at the dining room retrieving the camera, not letting Angie play hide the sausage. But her face immediately brightened and I was glad I'd said what I'd said. Besides, it was the truth.

She shifted forward and once again swallowed my penis all the way down her throat. Boy, could she suck! I should lift her to the bed, pleasure her as well. But I couldn't move a muscle. Every sinew of my being, physical and mental, was transfixed on Angie's mouth and what she was doing to me.

She rocked her head back and forth as she sucked up my pole. At the top she pumped up and down, just a few centimeters, pushing my foreskin down and off the head of my penis. Then she circled the soft underside of her tongue around and around and I was floating. It was if I was in a soft warm blanket, every part of my skin being caressed.

I should be pleasuring her. My mouth hungered to lick up and down her, to taste her, to feel her tremble with pleasure. But now she was plunging up and down, faster and faster. I could hardly breathe. She slowed. I got my lungs half-filled. Then she began to rotate as she slid up and down me. I teetered. If the back of her bed hadn't been supporting my calves, I would have fallen over.

Then her mouth was off.

"Angie!" I whispered. That was all I had air for. I took a deep breath, intending to invite her to the bed together.

But she gripped my balls with one hand, caressing them lightly. Her other hand began to slide up and down my pole. Her mouth returned to the top. She twirled her tongue around and around, sometimes sucking up and down as well. I felt a twinge deep inside.

"Angie! I'm coming!" I gasped to give her the chance to take her mouth off. But she removed her hand and sucked hard all the way down my pole and I exploded inside her mouth. She swallowed and licked as lightning shot up my spine. She sucked. My insides pumped uncontrollably. She sucked every last ounce out of me. My balls pumped and pumped, powerful pumps, pleasurable pumps. Pure, *pure* pleasure! Pumps from the base, right up the length of my pole!

I stopped pumping, but she was still sucking. I gently lifted her head up and off. I reached for her hand to pull her to the bed. It was her turn. Instead, I collapsed to the floor next to her and we both sat with our backs to the bed. I couldn't move a muscle.

"That was great!" I told her. As soon as my breathing returned to normal, I'd use the afterglow to probe about Underhill.

She shrugged. "Bernie said you needed sex." That completely killed the afterglow. I kissed her on the top of her head, got up and dressed. She got up without looking at me and went into the shower.

When she came out of the shower, I bent to kiss her. She offered her cheek. "You're a great lover," I told her.

"Thanks, Kyle. You're sweet." She stood on her tiptoes and gave me a light kiss on my lips. "See you at breakfast." I took that as my cue to leave.

The dining room was almost entirely empty. I did a quick detour to fix myself an ice cream cone and to satisfy myself that no one was watching. The camera was where I'd left it. I quickly palmed it and headed straight for my room.

The day's events went into my novel in the cloud. Tomorrow, the camera would go back to exactly the same spot. And tomorrow, I would activate it!

I collapsed onto my bed, visions of Angie dancing in my head. My eyes shut but she was still there, smiling. She…

Chapter 5 *Jackie*

Underhill had been extra nice to me since my return to the resort. He'd opened the door to the rental car and smothered me with a hug. I'd asked to go to my room to freshen up. What I'd really wanted was to check my computer for updated reports from Washington. But Underhill had been flying high and he'd carried me to the ocean instead, pausing only to insert a large piece of pineapple between my lips. He washed all the sweat from my body and plopped me in front of the fresh-water showers by the beach. One of his ladies brought me a simple one-piece dress with 'Hedonism II' emblazoned across the chest.

Dinner was celebratory—something good must have happened. At least good for Underhill. I kept trying to move towards the edges of his sycophants so that I could attempt to slip away. But Underhill's smothering attention kept me at the center of the table. All of this made me even more anxious to return to my room to connect with my team back in Washington. But least it took my mind off the fact I wasn't wearing any underwear.

Partway through dinner Joel slipped away carrying the laptop. It took all my willpower to tear my eyes off the laptop and smile at Bernie.

A few minutes later, Joel came back, minus the laptop, but carrying a large paper bag. He started to hand the bag to Bernie, but Bernie shook his head. "You do the honors."

Joel reached into the paper bag and called out Johnny's name. Johnny got a brand new shirt. The errand boy tossed his old shirt aside. The new one fit his skin like a glove as he buttoned it up. Then Lydia, the over-endowed blonde, got a new bikini. She got up on a chair, wiggled out of her old bikini and slid the new one on. Kyle got sandals.

Shaneese's new bikini was white and looked exotic against her dark brown skin. Instead of a bikini, Nara received a purple one-piece swimsuit. But it was so sheer as to not cover anything. Angie's new bikini was also purple. It looked designer expensive.

After the catcalls died down, Joel set a bra and panty set down in front of me. The panties were satin, the bra see-through lace. Both were red. I reached for them but Bernie shook his head. "Isn't there something else?" he asked.

Joel reached into the bottom of paper bag. His hand came

back up with a small jewelry box. I stifled a gasp. Surely Underhill's not going to propose!

"Open it," Bernie told Joel.

Inside were two gold nipple barbells. *Solid gold* nipple barbells. Even in the dim artificial light of the dining room, they gleamed, especially the little balls at the ends of each shaft. I leaned over, kissed Bernie's cheek, thanked him, and shut the lid of the jewelry box.

"Put them on," he told me.

I felt eight pairs of eyes lock onto my breasts. I crossed my legs; which reminded me that I wasn't wearing panties.

"Please," said Bernie, reaching for my breasts.

I gently moved his hands away and stood. First order of business was the panties up and under my dress. They were cool and smooth and soft and sensual. A frisson of electricity danced across my pussy.

Then I opened the lid of the jewelry box. The barbells were magnificent, so smooth and polished I could see my own reflection. I pulled the dress up and over my head. Sixteen eyes warmed my breasts. The warmth spread as chairs from the surrounding tables moved to allow for more to see.

I unscrewed the ball of the steel barbell from my left breast and put it in the jewelry box. Its worn steel looked pale next to the gold barbells Bernie was giving me. Then I unscrewed the ball from one of the gold shafts. I pressed it against the end of the old shaft which I used to guide the gold shaft into my breast. It felt fine, not like the discomfort I'd felt when I'd first inserted pins through my nipples. There was just a little scratchy-ness from the old and worn shaft. My nipple puckered slightly from the stimulation. A cheer erupted as I screwed the little gold ball into the shaft.

I unscrewed the steel ball from the other barbell and reached for the second gold one. But Bernie's fingers beat me to it. His fingers fumbled a bit around my nipple, engorging her hot and hard. *Everybody* in the dining room was watching. The jolts of electricity sparking around the jewelry being inserted into me made it hard to breathe. Finally Bernie had the new shaft in. But he fumbled even more screwing on the little gold ball. I had to steady myself against the table. Finally he stepped back.

This time the cheer was even louder and I felt I had to pirouette to give everyone a look. Every eye in the place was glued to my breasts. The cheer got even louder. I plopped down to my seat, my cheeks the color of the red bra which I quickly pulled on. Thankfully, at this point, everyone went back to their dinners and I was able to pull my dress back over my shoulders, tummy and thighs.

The last item in the bag was a gold bracelet for Joel.

I got up to refill my plate but Bernie took me by the hand and went with me to the buffet.

"Thank you for providing a much-needed distraction today," he whispered in my ear.

"I hope that that was the last of your tests." Yikes! Was that too sharp?!

But he put down our plates and pulled me aside. "That wasn't a test."

"Not a test?"

Bernie shook his head. "Shaneese and Nara said you passed." He was lying of course. But still it was nice that he'd made the effort. Something about my demeanor must have tipped him off that I wasn't buying it because he pulled my ear towards his lips. "Today, a special shipment came in. Multiple packages requiring individual attention, some large, some medium, some small. Your stunt meant that there was no one asking unnecessary questions during the offload."

Before he could see my reaction, I planted a large and slobbering kiss on his mouth. I had just helped him complete a major operation. If I didn't get some hard evidence to use against Underhill—and fast!—there would be hell to pay when I got back to Washington.

The rest of dinner was a happy affair, with Bernie spreading his considerable charm among his hangers-on and everyone glorying in the gifts they'd just received. Finally everyone had had enough and they leaned back in their chairs. The silence was broken only by stomachs rumbling to make room for dessert.

Underhill took me back to the buffet where he motioned to one of the servers and whispered something to him. A moment later, a man dressed in a chef's uniform came out with a tray atop of which were two large bowls of chocolate pudding with a smaller bowl of strawberries in the middle. The server came up from behind him, carrying two spoons. Underhill nodded at the spoons which were then added to the tray. He put his nose over one of the bowls and inhaled deeply. "Magnifico," he told the chef as he took the tray.

Underhill turned towards the exit. "Lead on," he told me. It was obvious that he meant that I should lead him to my room. I walked to his right, just slightly ahead. Steam rose from one of the bowls; the chocolate aroma was intoxicating.

Once I'd shut the door behind me, Bernie backed me up against it. His kiss was full of passion and desire. "Are you ready to have every inch of your body sucked and licked?" he asked.

I nodded. After the kiss, I was too out-of-breath to speak.

He pulled my dress up and over my head and carefully folded it. His eyes were on mine, dragging me into his intensity. I took quick shallow breaths, afraid to breathe deeply for fear that my breath might be cut off while I was still exhaling.

Bernie led me over to the dresser and pushed my legs against it. I couldn't sit or even lean back as the bowls of dessert were immediately behind me. He rubbed his body against mine, including the bulge in his crotch and I was forced to push back against him. His feral carnality penetrated my breasts and began to fuel cravings deep inside my sex. His kisses played with the lack of air inside my lungs.

Bernie dipped a finger into the hot pudding and held it in front of my lips. I carefully bent forward and touched my tongue to the tip of his finger. The chocolate was smooth and warm, sharp, not sweet.

"All of it," he told me.

I sucked the rest of the chocolate off and felt it enter my bloodstream. Clearly it had a very high cocoa content.

As my tongue licked the rest of the chocolate off my lips, Bernie dipped his finger into the other bowl. I tried to lap it off, but he pulled it away. He had my sex pressed against his leg, and my attempt to reach forward had rubbed it in a most pleasing way. Bernie moved his finger back and forth, letting me taste just a drop of chocolate each time. His eyes sparkled with the effect that his leg rubbing up and down between my thighs was having on me.

Finally, I put both my hands on the dresser, the tray between them, and leaned back. This drew Bernie's finger out of position. I pounced forward and sucked every last drop of chocolate into my belly.

Bernie's revenge for my trick was to use one of the spoons to put a dollop of pudding—cold!—on the tip of my nose and watch me shiver. As soon as I stopped shivering and took a deep breath, he flicked the pudding into his mouth with just the tip of his tongue.

Then he turned me around, facing the mirror and gently but firmly pulled my hair back over my shoulder. He reached around to dip his finger into the pudding and coated the outer rim of my ear with chocolate. "Don't shiver," he told me.

His tongue started at the bottom, softly licking off the chocolate. I trapped my shiver in the core of my body, and of course that made it worse. By the time he'd reached the top of my ear, I was shuddering uncontrollably.

Bernie chuckled at my discomfiture and pulled my hair up and over my other shoulder, exposing my entire neck.

Air blew against the back of my neck. I stomped my feet. "Stop that!" I told him.

"As you wish." His arm reached around in front of me. "Shut your eyes."

Since he could see me in the mirror, I had no choice and everything went black. Something landed on the back of my neck. Cold! My body shivered as it slid down. The shiver intensified as his tongue lapped the pudding back and forth at the base of my neck. Then I jerked ramrod stiff as he licked my neck clean with back and forth strokes all the way up to my hairline.

"You beast!" I yelled, then sucked air as deep into my lungs as I could manage.

"Stand still," he told me and I suddenly realized that I'd been gyrating my hips and undulating my back. I put my hands on the dresser to steady myself.

His hand reached around and removed a strawberry from the small bowl. He pressed the frigid fruit against the small of my back and I shuddered. "Stand still," he told me. I used his willpower to stand still—I couldn't have done it on my own.

The strawberry dragged its cold and rough surface up and down my spine, torturing my entire body into heightened arousal. Then he dragged it down my right thigh and tickled the back of my knee. I stamped my feet to make him stop.

"Stand still!" he demanded.

"Stop it!" I retorted. He touched the strawberry against my other knee. "Don't you dare!"

"Stand still."

It tickled uncontrollably, but I was able to stand still and was rewarded by tingles going up my thigh and into my sex. Bernie bit off half the strawberry and let me eat the other half. It was sweet and wet and juicy. I had never tasted anything so delightful!

A strong finger traced down the center of my back, then under the top of my panties. They pulled away from my skin.

"Like what you see?" I asked as I swayed my hips back and forth.

"Hot or cold?"

"Warm is always nicer."

"If you choose warm now, the next will be cold."

"The next?"

He released the back of my panties, slid his finger down my belly, and pulled the front of my panties forward. Cold? It wasn't touching, but I felt a cold bowl being held just below my tummy. "The next." His finger returned behind me and pulled the back of my panties forward. This time I kept my hips completely still. "Hot or cold?" he repeated.

"Cold."

The cold bowl disappeared. Something stabbed at the center of my back. I gasped. Then I took a deep breath to steady myself as cold pudding continued to dribble down. It flowed downward, downward. Under my panties. Into my butt crack, sometimes overflowing, chilling down and down, to the bottom of my butt crack. Frigid pudding threatened to seep into my pussy. I took a deep breath, relieved to see him returning the bowl to the right side of the tray.

But then he pulled by buttocks apart. Cold speared my most private spot and I whirled around.

"You bastard!" I yelled.

I stamped my feet as the pudding began to freeze the bottom of my pussy. He laughed uproariously and reached around me to the right side of the tray.

"Not that one, the other one!" I hissed.

Bernie shrugged and came back with the bowl of warm pudding. Blissful fragrances wafted up into my nostrils. He pulled my panties forward. As soon as the pudding started to flow, I spread my legs. It trickled down my pubic bone, over my clit and down my pussy, spreading wonderful warmth along the way. Where pudding met pudding, spring sunshine replaced frozen snow.

He kissed me then while lightly pulling up and down on the front of my panties. Warmth worked itself into every crevice and fold of my sex. I was floating. If he kept this up, I might come, just from the gentle pull and release of pressure of satin on skin.

But suddenly there was a clattering behind me and I realized I'd relaxed into the bowls on the tray. Bernie picked me up and laid me softly atop the bed. Pudding oozed back and forth into my sex and all over my butt. It leaked out onto the skin all along the edge of my panties. It was heavenly, both to feel and to watch in the mirror above the bed. I shut my eyes to savor the moment. Now all that we needed was for Bernie to—

Cold! On my nipples. My eyes flashed open. There, in the middle of my bra were two dollops of dark chocolate pudding! It seeped through the lace, freezing my nipples, then spreading out over my breasts.

"Bernie! How could you?!"

His head covered my breasts and I felt his mouth envelope my left nipple. He sucked the cold pudding off. It was *so* warm. My eyes fluttered, then shut. But then his mouth left for my other breast and warmth was replaced by chilly wetness on the nipple he'd abandoned. Once again warmth enveloped nipple and I could breathe. His mouth slowly lifted away and my right nipple had to fight back against the chill.

"Ready for another?" he asked.

"No!" I kept my eyes shut, daring him to defy me.

Pudding atop my nipples. "You bastard!" I yelled. My eyes flashed anger up to his, but all he did was to smile down at me.

"Are you sure?" he asked.

I realized that he'd used the warm pudding this time. It felt *so* soothing. I relaxed, enjoying the sensations. "You still have to lick it off," I told him.

His mouth vacuumed the pudding up and through my bra. My nipples almost followed. I leaned back as he gently licked away at the last droplets.

Then I felt fingers pull up on my panties. I propped myself up on my elbows. Bernie was readying to pour pudding down into my sex. "That better be warm!"

Bernie touched the bowl to my tummy. It was the warm one and I nodded. Pudding flowed into my sex. Flowed, filled and overflowed. I flopped back onto the bed and shut my eyes to concentrate on the sensations. He set the bowl down and tugged at the edges of my panties. First the top to caress the pudding into each nook and cranny of my pussy. Then the right side to stroke against my pussy lips.

His fingers released the right side and grabbed the top and the left side of my panties. This time he rotated and managed to brush the soaked satin over the top of my clit. The satin was barely touching her. Still, each gyration sent sparks up my spine.

Gradually the pressure on the front of my sex increased. I opened my eyes and looked up into the mirror. Bernie was pressing his hand against the front of my panties. As soon as I moaned, he started to stroke his fingers up and down the length of my sex. Each stroke shortened the length of my breath. Each stroke tightened and concentrated the pleasure roiling inside my sex. My whole body was on fire with desire for him! Each stroke was faster than the last. Each stroke sucked more and more of the air out of my lungs and into his fingers.

"Take me!" I pleaded, reaching for his cock.

But he pushed my hands away. "All in good time, my dear."

Then he slowed his strokes. I was stuck at maximum arousal but denied the release of orgasm. Rapture trapped me. Passion ensnared me. I was coated in infinite pleasure. But there was no escape.

"Bernie!"

"You want me to let you go?"

My sex, my entire middle, tightened, yearning for release. My pussy clenched, but couldn't climax. "Let me come. Bernie! Please!"

"You'll do anything for me. Won't you my pet?"

"Yes, Bernie. Yes! Please!"

"Anything I ask?"

"Yes! I'll do—"

His hand moved under my panties. I gasped. His finger dragged up the center of my pussy, wagging back and forth. I couldn't breathe. Just as I was about to pass out, his finger touched my clit.

My body wrenched sideways. Then, as soon as his hand left my sex, thrust upwards. Sideways again on the bed. Only then did I become aware of the rhythm of the contractions inside my sex and the waves of pleasures undulating up my spine. My toes tingled.

As my orgasm subsided, its delight turned into a thousand little feathers stimulating each cell of my body to its ultimate glory. Bernie dropped a dollop of chocolate into my mouth to complete my ecstasy. I lay motionless, powerless as he removed my lingerie and gently padded the remnants of the chocolate off my skin with a damp, and ever so warm, face cloth.

A tart cold strawberry, its juices dribbling down my cheek revived me. "Your turn," I told him.

Bernie lay flat on his back. I made a show of replacing the bowl of warm pudding on the bed with the cold one. He chuckled.

I lifted his briefs up and over his enormous erection. He had to be at least ten inches and he was as wide as a tree trunk. He was uncircumcised, but his arousal had pulled his foreskin down exposing the very purple head of his cock. Veins throbbed a deep red.

I dipped two fingers into the pudding and aimed for his nose. But a shake from his head held me in place.

"One each on my nipples, then suck me off," he said. "After that, it's your turn again.

I dabbed chocolate on each of his nipples, then circled my tongue around them until they were as clean as new. Then I turned my head to look down his body; it was time to go lower.

I dropped dollops of chocolate pudding all around the top of his cock. It throbbed as each one landed. Finally his whole shaft was shiny chocolate. I sucked the tip into my mouth, but I could only go down a few inches. Even so, he moaned appreciatively. Running my tongue around his cock just inside the lower edge of his foreskin provoked even deeper moans.

I licked back and forth along the base of his exposed glans. This area, the frenulum, is the quickest way to the male orgasm. Bernie groaned, but I couldn't really exert enough force to bring him off. His girth meant that I'd have to use my hands in addition to my mouth.

I carefully balanced myself so that I could use both hands at the same time. The chocolate made it easy to slide up and down his shaft and once again there was a loud groan of appreciation. He throbbed beneath my fingers as I slid them up and down. The throbs told me just how fast to caress him and how firmly to hold his shaft.

As I slid up and down his cock, I began to rotate my hands

around his girth. This brought forth sustained moaning. I felt wonderful repaying the pleasures Bernie had bestowed on me.

Every few cycles, I lifted my mouth off his shaft and slid my hands up and over the top of his cock. He absolutely adored this! And this brought new pudding onto the head of his penis that I licked and sucked off.

Bernie's cock was hot. Even when I used one of my hands to bring some of the cold pudding over, it was immediately warmed up. And it was hard. But the pudding lubricated my fingers as they slid over all the little bumps and ridges. Its throbbing told me to accelerate my strokes.

Faster and faster I went. Louder and louder he moaned. Up and over, round and round I slid my hands. He needed the most vigorous stimulation I could give him, so my mouth was mostly up and off. Which was good because bending over was strenuous and I was panting with the exertion.

His glans changed color to an even deeper purple and the throbbing inside his cock became more organized. He was about to come. I was going to make Bernie come!

The first spirt hit me on the forehead. I clamped my mouth onto the top of his cock. The second spirt hit the top of my throat, hot and hard. I sucked and sucked as spurt after spurt filled my mouth and I had to swallow. Bernie thrashed uncontrollably, but I moved with him and kept sliding my hand up and down his cock. I made sure to slide up and over his frenulum and touch the bottom of his now very tender glans with each stroke. He was mine! I wasn't going to let him escape.

Gradually he subsided and lay still. I continued to caress his cock until his breathing returned to normal. His eyes fluttered open. Finally there was a hint of softness in his erection.

Then I lifted my hands off his cock and looked straight into his eyes. They had a dreamy look with only a hint of their usual sparkle. I made a show of swallowing his semen. I didn't usually swallow, but with Bernie I wanted to get as much of him as possible. A smile of triumph crossed his face. A smile of complete possession, of absolute dominion. I smiled back in agreement.

Suddenly the feral look flashed back into his face. In one fluid motion he rose above me and turned me onto my back. I marveled at the complete lack of effort the maneuver had required.

Bernie picked up a pair of strawberries and raked them across my nipples. My back arched with the sudden pain. Then my pussy warmed towards the pleasure as he rotated the berries round and round my hardening buds.

Then one strawberry touched just above my clit and somehow I had to fall back to the mattress. The other berry squeezed juice into my mouth. Below, the first berry left my skin. Then its tip pressed into the center of my pussy. Bernie let me bite off the tip of the second berry, then squeezed even more juice into my mouth.

I opened my mouth wide and bit upwards but the berry above my mouth had disappeared. Below the other berry began to vibrate. I opened my mouth wide for another attempt. Suddenly my mouth was filled with the berry. I crushed it to flood my mouth with its tart sweetness. I was only dimly aware that the other berry had left my pussy.

Bernie's lips. His tongue! His tongue flicked up and down my pussy, spreading warmth, fluttering her lips, gushing her juices. His mouth sucked. Then lips and tongue and mouth together, kissing, licking, sucking, caressing, lapping, slurping.

Everything all together overwhelmed with its combined intensity and I almost blacked out. Then, without warning, my sex shuddered into orgasm. Bernie continued to kiss and lick and suck, spreading spasms of delight up and down my entire body. Undulating waves of warmth and excitement!

Then, just as my climax was receding, he lifted his mouth off. As smooth as water, Bernie rose above me, mounted his hips to mine and slid his cock inside me.

"Yes, Bernie," I exhaled.

Slowly, excruciatingly slowly, he pushed himself into me.

"Faster!" I urged.

"No, my pet, slow and sure!" He pulled himself out, just as slowly.

"Faster!"

"Relax, my pet—"

I arched my cunt into him, impaling myself on his cock. He gasped. I dropped myself down and he plopped out. "Faster!" I demanded.

And evil gleam took over the depth of his eyes. He plunged himself into me, then used his full weight, his full strength to pin me to the bed. "And harder?"

"Faster! Harder!" I beat my fists against his shoulders.

He raised his chest off me, but his pelvis still had me pinned against the mattress. "Faster? Harder?" he asked, his evil gleam slicing through my eyes and deep into my skull.

Danger bells sounded. But I didn't care. "Faster! Harder!" I cried.

And then he fucked me harder than I've ever been fucked before. It wasn't love. It wasn't sex. It was *fucking* pure and simple. A hard thrust. Pulling out to consume my control. Thrusting in to impose *his* control. Pulling out to suck me totally within his dominion. Thrusting to smash my will. Pulling out to suck me completely into his domain. Fucking. Fucking! *Fucking!*

Thrusting—no he was propelling me into the sky. White hot warmth. Floating. Pulsing. I was nothing. He was everything. Pulsing. Pulsing! *Pulsing!* I was in the thrall of a tornado, in the thrall of Bernie's maniacal laughter. I was in *heaven*!

Then my orgasm relaxed into a sumptuous feast of sensations. Little waves lapped against the sides of my pussy. Sparks swirled around my nipples. Each breath slid infinite smoothness from the top of my throat down to the bottom of my lungs.

Best of all was Bernie shuddering inside me. "Kiss me with your cunt!" he demanded. And I did, sending new pleasures thundering up our spines.

We journeyed together back and forth to the ends of time. Then he collapsed next to me on the bed. We weren't asleep, but we weren't talking either. Our bodies touched. We breathed in unison. I knew I needed to encourage Bernie to leave. I had a report to file. But I was powerless to take any action. All willpower, all self-determination, resided with him.

Finally Bernie pulled his body away from mine. All warmth left me. He left my room. I was numb, bereft, paralyzed.

At long last, with a great deal of effort, I dragged myself off the bed and logged into my F.B.I. portal. As best I could tell I had only three muscles that weren't aching.

First up was Kyle Fairbairn's criminal background. He'd started out with petty stuff, then graduated to bank robbery. He'd been caught and done a stint in Millhaven, one of Canada's most notorious penitentiaries. After release, he'd worked as a 'security consultant' for several questionable organizations. One of these assignments led to him being investigated, but never charged, for murder. The heat from the murder investigation had rendered Kyle unemployable in Canada, so he'd branched out internationally and had ended up in Underhill's crew a few months ago.

More interestingly, the report disclosed that Kyle's real name was Keith Martin and that he was a former Royal Canadian Mounted Police Officer. However, the Canadians hadn't passed very much onto the F.B.I.—our file on him said only that he was on paid medical leave. There was no official record of a 'Kyle Fairbairn' alias. Given Martin's current activities "paid medical leave" must be what the Mounties were putting out for public consumption. It was more likely that Martin/Fairbairn had been suspended or even discharged for dishonorable conduct.

So, Martin must have come up with the Kyle Fairbairn persona on his own. Faced with the loss of his paycheck, not to mention his pension, he'd been in need of some quick cash. Had he sought out Underhill or had it been the other way around? Maybe he'd been working for Underhill for years. In any event, however it had happened, Keith Martin/ Kyle Fairbairn was no longer an upstanding citizen.

Other than what the Mounties had sent us, there was no record of Keith Martin ever having existed. Someone had done a good job of erasing him.

I started to craft plans to sabotage Kyle. It would weaken and disrupt Underhill's operation. And if I got credit for it, Underhill's confidence in me would deepen. But it would be risky for Bernie to know that I was behind the sabotage. It would have to be done carefully and at the right time.

There was also some background on Angie—Angela Connors. Underhill had apparently "rescued" her from a human smuggling operation. From all accounts it was one of his own operations. But Angie wouldn't know that. The public records had her working at a hotel at the time. I sighed. Angie had been with Underhill for some time, and her gratitude would make it almost impossible to get her to testify against him.

But the kicker was an update on a piece of new technology the Bureau planned to test on Underhill: an antenna designed to intercept pre-encrypted WiFi communications in a form which would immediately duplicate the screen content of all parties to the communications.

I filed a quick update, describing my trip into Montego Bay and Underhill's expression of gratitude. I left out the fact that, for the first time in my life, I'd swallowed another man's semen.

My report ended with a quick query back to my team back in D.C. asking for their input on whether exposing Kyle might bring me closer into Underhill's confidence. But the team back in Washington would have to come up with a cover story as to how I'd managed to discover Kyle Fairbairn's true identity.

I sat staring into my screen for some time as I fidgeted with a flash drive memory key. Then my chin hit my chest and I had to jerk my head back. I quickly logged out of my computer, hid the memory key, and dragged myself to the shower. It was time for hot jets of water to cleanse my body of the remnants of the chocolate pudding clinging to it. Even more, I needed to wash away Underhill's deepening hold over me.

Chapter 6 *Kyle*

Breaking into Johnny's room was risky, but I knew he'd be doing his early morning sweep for surveillance devices in the dining room. If I were to be caught, I would claim that I was doing routine surveillance, like any good head of security would. I just hoped that I'd never have to find out how far that excuse might get me. Something big had gone down yesterday; I needed a clue as to what it might have been.

The fact that Lydia was still in Johnny's bed certainly increased the chances of being caught. I kept one eye on her as I padded around the room, glad for the extra ninja training I'd had. She slept on her tummy. Her round rump was completely white. If she woke, I'd give her a spanking and tell her that one night with Johnny had been fine, but another without Underhill's specific permission might get her thrown off the island. She'd keep her mouth shut for sure.

Johnny's mother had never taught him to be neat. Clothes were strewn on every available surface. Papers were also here there and everywhere. Receipts for food; Underhill demanded daily deliveries of goat yogurt. Receipts for a rental car. Lists of things Underhill needed for travel. Travel brochures.

Lydia stirred. Ninja silence or no, I'd have to leave soon. There! In the corner. A stack of papers.

Jackpot! All nice neat stapled together. A Bill of Lading for an international shipping container. Processing documents for the port of Montego Bay. A receipt for an outgoing shipping container. I flipped back and forth between the documents. There were two *different* containers. The date was yesterday. One, or maybe even both containers might still be in port.

I locked Johnny's door behind me and did my best to nonchalantly stroll to the dining room. But my mind was racing to come up with an excuse to go into Montego Bay. I just *had* to check out those containers. If they held even just one piece of corroborating evidence! I cursed my lack of a connection inside the Jamaican Constabulary.

At the dining room, Johnny was wearing a tennis outfit. Damn—I'd forgotten that Underhill had decreed that today was tennis day. A 'beep' told Johnny that his search wand had been operating properly. He turned it off and slipped it back into his case as I came up behind him. "Everything okay?" I asked.

He looked up and down my long sleeved shirt and full-length trousers. "How come you're not dressed for tennis? I reserved the courts for right after breakfast."

"I'll change later."

The ladies skipped and scampered into the dining area. Their tennis outfits were all on the very skimpy side, Jackie's and Angie's the skimpiest. A moment later Underhill strode in. Like me, he was wearing shirt and trousers. Joel was behind him, also in street attire.

Underhill let the ladies prance around in their tennis outfits for several minutes. Then he clapped his hands. "Change of plans. No tennis. We're going cliff diving at Rick's."

Everyone was momentarily disappointed, then excited. Rick's Café was an institution in these parts. We'd been hearing rumours about the spectacular view off Jamaica's west coast and the thirty-five foot high cliffs off which the adventurous dove.

Damn! How was I going to get into Montego Bay?! Rick's was down the road in the opposite direction.

In the middle of a sigh of resignation, Underhill waved me over. "Kyle, I want you to stay behind. I've received reports, unclear and vague, but solid. Something's going to happen here today. Keep your eyes open." He handed me a small underwater camera, the type that works above and below the surface. "Take pictures of everything you see."

I started to thank my lucky stars. But Underhill hadn't finished. "I want you to go on both snorkel cruises. Take pictures from the boat. Under and above the water."

I nodded. "When will you be back?"

"For dinner. Make sure no one takes our tables."

As soon as everyone piled into the minivan which would take them to Rick's, I got on the phone to arrange a flight to Montego Bay. Taking one of the single-engine prop planes favored by upper-class tourists would be the only way for me to get back and forth from Negril to Mo Bay and still have time to investigate Underhill's shipping container. Just then one of the single-propeller planes roared overhead. I slammed down the receiver and caught a cab to the landing strip.

Three hours later, I boarded the plane for the return trip to Negril. The landing strip was five minutes from Hedo. I would have just enough time to change into swimming trunks, dash down to the beach and jump into the small boat which would take us out to the reef to snorkel.

I had found the incoming shipping container, but by the time I'd arrived, it had been scrubbed clean and was half filled with a new cargo. The outgoing container had been loaded on another ship. But the port's records had had a gap in them and I had been unable to ascertain the identity of the outgoing vessel.

There didn't seem to be anything out of the ordinary at resort. I took several photos going out to the reef, toggling the camera back and forth between eleven am and 2 pm. I did the same while snorkeling. I hoped the shots were turning out—the LED screen was black under the bright Jamaican sun. One would have thought that the camera's manufacturer would have made a brighter screen.

I got fellow snorkelers to take two shots of me in my red swim trunks. One with the shore in the background, the other facing the sea would hide the fact that the sun was in the west for both shots.

On the way back, I also toggled the time on my camera back and forth, except now a full half-an-hour later. But now something was going on. A crew was installing an antenna array. I made sure that the "morning" shots didn't show the antenna.

In my room, I had a quick shower to wash off the salt water. Then I popped the camera's SD card into my computer. Fifteen minutes later, I'd altered the image numbers on the photos to follow the same sequential order as the clock time they'd been recorded with. Unless Joel did a deep, deep search, it would appear as if I'd followed Underhill's orders and gone out for both the morning and afternoon snorkel cruises.

Dinner was just being set up when I approached the dining room. Neither Underhill nor anyone from his entourage was present.

So I strolled over to the reception desk. A woman neatly dressed in a red Hedo shirt smiled at me. "So," I asked, "does this mean we're going to get better internet speeds?"

"Are you having a problem with your WiFi?"

"No, but it could be faster. Isn't that why they were putting in the new antenna?"

"No, that is for the telephone company."

"What service?"

She shrugged. "Telephone. We have to allow their equipment."

I thanked her and left. I didn't think that pressing her would net me any more information. All it would accomplish would be for her to remember the conversation.

I strolled around to have a look at the antenna. It was ensconced unobtrusively behind the kitchen. Unless you knew where to look, you wouldn't notice it.

Back in the dining room, I watched women stroll in. Most were in the company of a male companion. A pang of regret made my heart skip a beat. I hadn't had a relationship with a woman that had lasted for more than three weeks since my engagement with Sally had broken off five years ago.

A single woman wandered by. She was tall and blonde, wearing a bikini. Attractive and fit. *And* she was my age. If I weren't on the job, I'd amble over and have a go at chatting her up. 'On the job', was that just an excuse? Her buttocks squeezed and released as she made her way to the buffet. Another woman, an equally attractive brunette was approaching—

Enough self-torture for one day. I made my way back to the office and it's public computer. Five minutes later I wished I hadn't bothered. The only item in my inbox had been an invitation to meet with the R.C.M.P.'s supervening conduct authority early next week. Such invitations were almost always the harbinger of bad news. The usual outcome of this type of meeting was the scheduling of an early disciplinary hearing.

Chapter 7 *Jackie*

After Underhill's surprise announcement of a trip to Rick's Café, we all dashed back to our rooms to replace our tennis shirts and skirts with ordinary resort attire. Ten minutes later, Underhill bundled us all into the minivan he'd rented for the occasion.

Underhill sat up front and was immediately the center of attention of his four women. Joel and Johnny sat in the middle, occasionally chatting. Outside the minivan, Kyle, Underhill's security chief, kept watch over the vehicle. A big strong man like that would be nice to cuddle up next to after passions had been stoked and satisfied. He was a strange one, but it was a pity we hadn't met at another place, in another time.

The road to Rick's was typical of Jamaica: winding, the odd farm animal, the odd small house or shop, lots of greenery, cars speeding towards or away. There was more drama up front, albeit drama of the predictable kind. But after experiencing Underhill up close and personal, I understood the attraction. The man could certainly weave a spell.

When I was next to him, my professionalism had evaporated. I had completely torpedoed my credibility. No jury would believe me. Convicting Underhill would now require hard evidence. My role on the stand would be restricted to connecting the dots.

Maybe it would be better if I was married, if I had a solid connection outside the job. As it was, I did whatever the job required. And I did it in the moment. Others, who weren't in the field, would criticize me later. My only protection against their censure would be having Underhill behind bars.

I watched the women fawning over him. Even Nara, who was so strong and independent when she was outside his presence, was practically swooning as she rubbed his chest. I sighed; if the Asian woman couldn't resist Bernie, what hope was there for me?

Finally, we arrived at Rick's. The Café was arranged in a semi-circle. Bernie told Johnny to get us drinks. I ordered a Guinness, a beer not available at Hedonism.

At one end was the cliff. One or two people were jumping off. Some appeared to be having fun. Others looked terrified.

Bernie was next to Joel, gesturing towards the diving board. "You have to jump," he told his assistant.

"I don't think so."

"Be a man."

"If I'm injured, the transaction will unravel."

A large white male, somewhat overweight, jumped forward. Joel and Bernie craned their necks to watch him smash into the water. The ocean closed back over where he had entered. Joel began to look concerned.

Then the diver's head broke the surface of the water. Bernie slapped Joel's shoulder. "See, piece of cake!"

Bernie quickly slipped out of his shirt and pants and handed them to Angie. He was now wearing only swim trunks. He stepped up to the cliff and pointed to Joel: "I expect to see you in the water."

And then he went over the cliff. A moment later, he popped to the surface and waved.

Nara nudged Joel. "Aren't you going to jump?"

Joel shook his head.

Nara shrugged, pulled her T-shirt over her head and dropped her skirt. She was wearing a white bikini. Nara stepped to the platform and disappeared over the edge.

Joel watched the water below. As soon as Nara's head popped to the surface, he swore, stripped off his outer clothes, strode to the diving board, and jumped over the edge.

Below, Bernie loudly congratulated his fellow adventurers. When Nara climbed out of the water, she was nude.

Several hours later, full of munchies, beer, and Rick's special drinks, our minivan returned us to Hedonism. At dinner, those of us who ate, only ate lightly. Underhill waved Kyle over and held out his hand. Kyle gave him a small camera which Underhill handed to Joel.

"Did you see anything?" asked Bernie.

Kyle nodded. "The telephone company installed an antenna of some sort."

"Which company?"

"The lady at the front desk didn't seem to know. She didn't seem to think that the resort had any choice but to allow the installation." Kyle seemed to be dividing his attention between Bernie and what Joel was doing with the camera. Several photos flashed on Joel's computer screen, then a long scrolling list.

"Did you take pictures of the antenna?" asked Bernie.

Kyle nodded and pointed to the camera.

Bernie tapped Joel on the shoulder. "Everything alright?"

Joel nodded. "Both trips, morning and afternoon."

"Show me the photos of the antenna."

All three men huddled over Joel's screen. "Do you know what that is?" Bernie asked.

Joel nodded, "It's a—"

Bernie jiggled Joel's shoulder, this time quite roughly. "That was a 'yes' or 'no' question. Can you fix it?"

"Yes."

"Good. Let me know when you're finished."

Uncharacteristically, everyone seemed tired and one-by-one we left the dining room. When I left, Lydia, the big-breasted blonde, was enjoying being the sole focus of Underhill's attentions.

Up in my room, I established a secure videophone link with my boss back in Washington, D.C.

"Did the WiFi interceptor antenna work?" I asked.

"For all of ten minutes. First there was an added layer of encryption. It'd take years to crack that stuff. Then the WiFi signal was blocked completely."

"Shit!"

"My sentiments exactly."

"And now he'll be even more careful."

"Yes, I'm sure we've spooked your Mister Underhill."

"*My* Mister Underhill?!"

"Yes, *your* Mister Underhill. He's become an obsession with you. We have other targets which are more imminent threats to national security. I want you back up here tomorrow to start dealing with them. Nancy will be taking over the pursuit of Mr. Underhill." Nancy was a bumbler who'd have difficulty pursuing her own shadow.

"Wait!" I told him. "Underhill is about to pull of a big score. Give me another week."

There was a pause. "You can have until Monday. I want you back in the office first thing Tuesday for an important meeting regarding your next target. Your *more important* target."

The screen went blank but I continued to stare at it. Unless I made something happen tomorrow, or at the latest the day after, Underhill would go free.

Chapter 8 *Kyle*

The next evening, I was sitting in the dining room with Underhill, Jackie, and the rest of his entourage. We were all lounging in our chairs, waiting for the evening's entertainment to start. And that's what my investigation was doing, lounging. Next week, Underhill would leave the resort and I'd have to return to Ottawa to meet my professional fate. If I went back up north empty-handed, my chances of leaving the force with my pension intact were fifty-fifty at best.

Underhill was in the middle of a story and I decided it was best to tune in. "…The guide held up his hand for us to stop. Everyone went completely silent. There was a rustle in the undergrowth to our left. Suddenly—"

Beep! It was Underhill's phone. He signaled for Joel to open the laptop. The two men huddled over the screen. Joel typed frantically, then paused. Both men gestured at the screen.

The women let out a collective sigh. They were all dressed as groupies. Hedo's costume theme for the night was 'Rock Star'. Joel wore tight jeans and a Rolling Stones T-shirt. Johnny sported KISS regalia. Underhill was resplendent in a one-piece spandex outfit. Its shiny gold hugged his body and emphasized every aspect of his manhood. Angie and Lydia were both sexy in short skirts and blouses barely large enough to accommodate their breasts. Shaneese was wearing white spandex, Nara black.

Jackie's jeans had more holes than denim. Her tube top left her tummy bare. She wasn't wearing a bra.

The women were just starting to get fidgety when the show started. They settled back to watch a live band play a medley of Bob Marley standards. Underhill and Joel were still consumed by whatever was on their laptop. I divided my attention between them and the show. Out of the corner of my eye, I thought I saw Jackie watching Underhill, but when I turned towards her, her eyes were focused on the stage.

Me, I was fidgety for another reason. For the evening's theme, I had gone to the gift shop to purchase one of their pre-packaged costumes. It had looked better on the packaging than it had when I'd inspected myself in the mirror. The black tights looked somewhat silly on my oversized body. And they were uncomfortable. At least I was able to leave the shirt unbuttoned to show off all the fake bling which had come with the kit. The reggae band was more than half way into its medley before I found a comfortable seating position.

When the band started into one of its own compositions, the women got restless and start chattering among themselves. Johnny escaped by going to get drinks.

Lydia pointed to the laptop. "Work, work, work," she muttered, but loud enough for Joel and Underhill to hear.

"No play," said Angie.

"Makes Bernie a dull boy," finished Shaneese.

Nara glared daggers in the direction of the laptop. Jackie looked back and forth between Underhill and the women, as if seeking an opening.

Underhill pointed to the laptop and told Joel to, "Do it."

Just then Johnny returned with a tray full of a variety of drinks, many colorful, two with paper umbrellas poking out of them. Underhill took the tray and played waiter, correctly guessing what each person wanted. Joel shut the laptop. There was a disorganized milling about. Everyone was vying for Underhill's attention, but in a good-natured way because they were all glad that he'd returned to the party.

Underhill held up a small glass of amber liquid. It had large orange peel in it. "And the best Jamaican rum for Mr. Ritchie." Joel took the cocktail. Underhill raised something similar and both men clinked their glasses together.

"What should we do tonight?" asked Underhill.

"Spin the bottle," said Lydia.

"Key party," said Joel.

"Strip poker," contributed Jackie.

"Strip Blackjack," said Johnny.

"Truth or Dare," said Nara.

"Talent night," suggested Angie.

I offered, "Roll the dice."

"Blindfold touching," offered Shaneese. This was a game where one person was blindfolded and then touched and fondled by everyone else. The person blindfolded had to guess who was doing the touching and fondling.

Everyone looked expectantly towards Underhill. As always, the choice would be his. "Not dice or talent. Blackjack is too complicated. Key party requires an even balance—"

Joel raised his hand. "Not if Johnny and I choose first."

Underhill shook his head. "Truth or Dare, Strip Poker, Spin the bottle."

The women started shouting. It quickly came down to Strip Poker or Spin the bottle.

"What's she doing with the laptop?" said Lydia. Jackie looked to be touching Joel's laptop.

But everyone else was still competing over the game. "Strip Poker," shouted Angie and Joel. "Spin the Bottle," responded Shaneese, Johnny and Nara. I joined in the chant for strip poker.

"What's she doing with the laptop?" shouted Lydia.

Everyone went silent and looked at Lydia. She pointed at Jackie who was edging sideways away from the computer. "She put something in the laptop."

"A memory key?" asked Joel.

"Could be," nodded Lydia. "She stuck it right in the side." Lydia made a motion as if inserting a flash drive into the side of a laptop.

Jackie held up her hands. They were empty. She shook her head.

Underhill looked back and forth between the two women. Then he gestured for me to go to Jackie. "Search her!"

Jackie looked as if she was about to make a run for it. But Johnny was blocking her way. So she made a show of standing her ground and spreading her legs.

Jackie's body was warm, muscular and fit. She seemed nervous. Tucked in a small slit the back of her jeans was a very thin memory key. I palmed it and continued my search by patting up and down her legs. As I stood, I managed to drop the memory key into my pocket. I moved behind her and patted her tube top.

"A thorough search," demanded Underhill.

I squeezed her breasts. They were firm and I could feel her nipple piercings.

"More," demanded Underhill. He was looking into Jackie's eyes and she was returning his gaze. It was as if she was consenting to him searching her, as if I was a mere extension of Underhill's will.

I slipped my hands under her tube top. Her breasts were warm. My fingers tingled when I rubbed her engorged nipples. She gasped, but the gasp was for Underhill, not me.

"Maybe she put it inside her pants."

I pulled her zipper down. "Nothing there," I told Underhill.

"Take them off and check them thoroughly."

I pulled her jeans to the floor, then lifted them up, making a show of pressing every centimeter between my fingers.

I stepped back from Jackie, but Underhill waved me forward. "Check her panties."

I reached forward.

"Inside or out?" she asked, looking at me. My hand stopped an inch away from the top of her panties.

"Both," said Underhill.

Her panties were soft cotton, thin and smooth from having been worn repeatedly. Nothing there. Similarly, I found nothing when I slipped my hand inside to run it lightly over her buttocks.

She moaned when I put my fingertip under the front of her panties. "Make it a *thorough* search," she demanded. She spread her legs. In case I'd missed her meaning.

Jackie was warm and soft. Her outer lips opened, then caressed my finger. She moaned as I tapped lower. Without meaning to, I slipped my finger inside. She was warm and wet. Before I knew it, most of my finger had slipped inside. I quickly jerked it out.

"Lick it off," she told me.

I settled for wiping my finger off on a napkin before turning to Underhill. "She's clean, boss."

Everyone turned to Lydia. Underhill fixed her with a particularly hard stare. "I don't like liars," he told her.

"I saw her," insisted Lydia, fixing her blue eyes on Underhill's.

I rubbed my fingers up and down the surface of the memory key. I should have given it to Underhill, turned Jackie in. It would have cemented my relationship with the gangster. Instead of making the safe play, the sure play, I'd gone for the long shot, hoping against hope that there'd be something on the memory key. Something I could use to incriminate Underhill.

Underhill turned to Jackie. "What did you do?"

"Nothing! I swear!" She wanted to look at me, but she kept her eyes on Underhill.

The entourage was looking back and forth between the two women, Jackie shorter with long black hair, Lydia taller and blonde.

I should have made the safe and sure play. This type of boneheaded long shot was the reason my life—professional *and* personal—was in the crapper. This whole mission had been a long shot. Not turning Jackie in was a long shot within a long shot. I should have made the safe play. Instead, Underhill's vile criminal network would almost certainly continue after my career disintegrated next week.

"I saw her!" maintained Lydia.

Jackie shook her head. "How can you see what's not there?!"

"I don't like liars," said Underhill.

Jackie and Lydia spoke in unison. "She's the liar—"

Underhill's raised hand stopped them in mid-sentence. He pointed back and forth between Lydia and Jackie. "Either 'fess up right now, or suffer the penalty." He pointed to Lydia, "If I don't find anything on her, you'll get flogged." Then he turned to Jackie. "And if I do, you'll suffer the same consequence. And worse." He looked back and forth between the two women.

Neither said anything.

Underhill motioned to Jackie's top. She took it off and respectfully handed it to him. He pressed each centimeter between thumb and forefinger, then tossed it aside. He pointed to her panties. She stepped out of them and, using both her hands, gave them to Underhill. He held them between the thumb and forefinger of his right hand, then bounced them up and down. Finding nothing, he tossed them towards her top.

Everyone, especially Underhill, took a moment to enjoy Jackie's nudity. Her chest rose and fell with each breath causing the tail of the salamander tattoo to wrap itself around her right breast. Her tummy was flat and smooth, but the muscles beneath it made it clear that she could rock her hips, in the naughty dance, should anyone be lucky enough to get that close. And her hips—they were wide and full and fertile. All of this, and her round rump, were amply supported by long sexy legs. Aware of the attention being lavished on her, Jackie flicked her long black hair over her shoulder, jiggling her breasts suggestively. She cocked her hips to the right, exposing the snout of the salamander and making it look as if it was trying to lick her pussy.

Underhill stepped into Jackie, gripped her chin, then pressed back on her forehead. He stared into her mouth. "Lift your tongue," he told her.

Jackie almost gagged.

Underhill released her and Jackie started to swallow. Underhill hit her between her breasts with the palm of his hand. Jackie choked forward, but nothing came out of her mouth. She wobbled, trying to regain breath and balance.

Lydia looked concerned. Jackie stared defiantly back at Underhill. She was truly beautiful. And sexy. I felt a stirring within my rock star outfit. Warm, but very, very uncomfortable!

Angie lifted her lips to my ear and pointed to Lydia. I reluctantly tore my eyes away from Jackie as Angie whispered, "Lydia doesn't care, she's a masochist through and through."

Underhill took Jackie by the hair and pulled her head towards the floor. "Bend over and spread your legs." She complied. I wished I were standing behind her.

Underhill slapped Jackie's butt. The sound was loud. Thankfully the music from the stage was louder and it was only Underhill's entourage watching Jackie. "Don't move until I say so," Underhill told her.

Underhill spat on his finger, then pressed it forward between Jackie's legs. Jackie let out a loud groan and almost fell over. Underhill pulled his hand back. This time Jackie had to use her hands on the floor to steady herself. Underhill reached out his finger. Johnny poured his drink over it. Underhill wiped it clean with a napkin, pulling it down the length of his digit with a rotating motion.

Underhill looked at Jackie, then at me. "She's clean," he said. He slapped Jackie's butt, but not as hard this time. "Stand up."

Jackie gingerly raised herself up to standing. She looked around, located her clothes and quickly pulled them on.

Underhill pointed at Lydia. "You. To the Romping Room."

I raised an eyebrow. We hadn't reserved that facility. "Do you want me to—"

Underhill shook his head. "I don't care who sees." His face was severe. Lydia tried to look demure but in a tight pink blouse and red miniskirt, this was difficult.

Joel left with the laptop. Underhill led the rest of us to the Romping Room, making sure to keep Lydia in front of him.

In the Romping Room, Underhill grabbed Lydia's blonde hair and led her to the large purple room. There he tied her wrists to the chains dangling from the ceiling. She was standing atop a thin mattress and had to adjust her footing. At that moment Joel returned carrying an athletic bag. Underhill nodded to him and pointed to Lydia's feet. "She'll need a spreader."

Joel fished inside his bag and came back with a two-an-a-half foot long metal rod. It was thin and painted black. Cuffs were attached at both ends and these he fastened to Lydia's ankles. This had the effect of spreading her feet wide and pulling her arms tightly upward where they were bound to the chains suspended from the ceiling. It also had the effect of stretching the buttons on her blouse to their breaking point. I caught glimpses of her bra.

Underhill looked around the room. He motioned for Angie and I to sit on a red and black sawhorse type contraption. Everyone else was standing. Jackie was off to one side. I could see her face, but most of the others were in front of us.

When Underhill was satisfied that everyone had a good view, he turned to Lydia. "Are you ready to admit you were lying?"

Lydia shook her head and fixed her eyes on Jackie. "I *wasn't* lying." Brown and blue eyes jostled for advantage.

"Prepare her." It was Underhill's voice, but I had been watching Lydia and hadn't seen to whom he was talking.

Nara stepped forward, reached up to the top of Lydia's pink blouse and pulled. All the buttons popped loose. Lydia's black bra swayed back and forth under the burden of her breasts. Hard nipples, surrounded by large pink areolae, struggled to poke through the thin lace material. The Japanese unclasped her skirt, ripped it asunder, and let the thin material fall to the mattress. Lydia's panty was loose and made of the same material as her bra.

Nara reached for the space between Lydia's breasts, apparently having difficulty ripping the cups apart. Her hands fondled the blonde's nipples. Lydia pulled away, but her effort seemed to lead only to even more fondling.

Then Lydia stood still. "It has a clasp in front, bitch."

Nara pulled the clasp forward and inspected it. She let it drop back in place. Lydia's breasts jiggled inside the bra. Next Nara tugged at Lydia's thin black panties pulling them into her genitals. The motions made by Nara's hands made it clear that she was intent on arousing Lydia. The look on Lydia's face showed that Nara was succeeding.

"Enjoying yourself?" taunted Lydia.

"Not as much as you, bitch."

Nara let go of the panties and gave the blonde's genitals a sharp tap.

"Ow! Bitch!" yelped Lydia. "How dare you!"

"Say one more word and I'll show you how I dare."

Lydia clamped her lips shut but her eyes glared daggers at her tormentor.

Nara reached her hand out. Joel gave her a long knife. She twisted it, using the light to inspect its blade.

A single Japanese hand inserted the blade between Lydia's breasts. "Don't move, don't breathe," Nara told her.

Lydia stood completely still.

Nara's hand jerked sharply upwards. Lydia's bra cups flew outward. Her nipples begged to be touched. Lydia took a deep breath, extending her nipples ever further forward.

Nara began to fondle Lydia's panties. One finger, then two disappeared between the blonde's legs.

"Are you—"

"Shhh," said Nara. She raked the knife backwards down Lydia's leg. There wasn't any danger of cutting her skin, but the motion made it clear just how sharp the knife was. Lydia immediately quieted.

Nara slipped a hand under Lydia's panties and stroked her pubic prominence. "You're my bitch, aren't you, Lydia?"

Lydia remained silent.

Nara's hand went further down. "You're my bitch, Lydia. Say it!"

Lydia merely glowered.

Nara's hand went in further, her knuckles disappearing. "Say it."

Lydia moaned but shook her head. Nara used the knife to cut away at the black lace panties. They fell to the mattress and we could all see that Nara had two fingers up Lydia's vagina. "Say it!" demanded Nara.

Lydia shook her head.

Nara took the knife handle and inserted it into Lydia's sex. Almost to the hilt. "You're my bitch! Say it!"

"No!"

"Say it or I'll use the other end of the knife."

"You wouldn't dare!"

Nara took the knife handle out and turned the knife around. Lydia looked over to Underhill. "Bernie! She can't!"

Underhill shrugged.

Nara edged the knife closer and closer. Johnny tried to step forward, but Underhill held him back.

Lydia's eyes went as wide as saucers. The knife was almost touching. Jackie looked away.

"No!" screamed Lydia. Her whole body was quivering.

Nara held the knife rock steady. "Say it." Her voice was low, threatening.

"Bitch! I'm your bitch!" cried Lydia.

"Again!" Nara's eyes were ferocious, daring Lydia to give her a reason.

"I'm your bitch!"

"Again!"

"I'm your bitch!" Lydia was half sobbing, half standing defiant. Her body was aroused, sexually and ready for combat. Muscles rippled from her thighs to her shoulders.

"Enough," whispered Underhill.

Nara immediately relaxed. She handed the knife, handle first, to Joel. Joel gripped it strongly, then remembered where it had been moments before.

Underhill reached into Joel's bag and came out with a cat-o-nine-tails. He turned the whip over and over. It was obviously finely crafted. Each of the nine strands had a knot tied at the end. Where they met the handle, a shiny chrome ring bound them together. There was another chrome ring at the bottom of the handle. Johnny and Joel's eyes fixated on the whip as if its supernatural force prevented them from looking away. Jackie and Angie had turned away. Lydia and I were trying to look away but couldn't quite keep from looking at the whip as its handle sparkled in the light.

"Who wants to do the honours?" asked Underhill.

Johnny and Joel's right hands shot to the ceiling.

Underhill smiled. "We'll let the whip decide." He twirled it between its hands and the strands flew out in a perfect circle. Suddenly he stopped its spin. Most of the strands flopped down in Johnny's direction. Joel's shoulders slumped.

Underhill handed the whip to Johnny who slapped its strands lightly against his palm. Lydia shivered.

I bent towards Angie's ear. "We should stop this," I told her.
"You don't like watching sex?" she whispered back.
"Sex should be about pleasure, not pain."
"Sex should be about sex."
Underhill grabbed the top of the whip, forcing Johnny to look into his eyes. "Make it good or I'll have to finish her off."
Johnny swallowed and nodded. Underhill released the whip. Johnny took up position behind Lydia. The whip cracked against her flesh. Her whole body tensed. Pain showed on her face. The whip cracked again and again. She began to relax. A thin smile began to play around her lips.
"See, I told you she likes it," whispered Angie. Angie's body next to mine reminded me how uncomfortable my tights were. Every time she adjusted her position, the stirring below tightened painfully against my pants.
Johnny continued to whip the blonde. When we caught glimpses of him from behind Lydia's back, his expression was a mixture of lust, arousal and concern for his victim.
Lydia took a crack across her bottom. "Ow!" she protested. Jackie cringed.
"Harder!" demanded Underhill, a sadistic gleam sparkling in his eyes.
The next crack across her bottom was even louder than the one before. But instead of protesting, Lydia stared defiantly at Underhill.
In addition to our group, several other resort guests had gathered at this end of the room. They were staring, fascinated, at the proceedings. Lydia intermittently made eye contact with them or thrust her hips in their direction. She basked in their attention, using it to fuel her arousal.
Angie stroked her hand across my nipples. Then she rubbed between my legs. When I squirmed with the discomfort of my reaction to her ministrations, she pulled my tights down, then up and over my enthusiastic erection. She pulled them further down and my bum touched the soft but cold leather of the bench. At least no one seemed overly interested in my gonads. Angie's hand began to stroke up and down my penis, keeping time with Johnny's whip.
Underhill looked over and gave a brief, but approving, nod before turning his attention back to the woman being whipped.
Sweat provided a sexy sheen to Lydia's body. Her blonde

hair was beginning to mat. But her face showed that she was floating on the endorphins flooding into her bloodstream. Lydia was glorying in the moment, glorying in the devotion of those watching.

Johnny's whipped cracked. Angie's hand caressed.

Underhill began to clap his hands in time with Johnny's strikes. Then several joined in. The people behind us clapped. Finally, even Jackie was clapping. Lydia squirmed with each strike of the whip.

Angie wasn't clapping, but she was keeping time with Johnny's strikes. "Pinch my tits," she said. I undid a few buttons and slipped my hand under her blouse. Her nipples were hard, easy to find. I pinched. She shuddered and groaned with delight.

We were all whipping, being whipped.

Underhill stopped clapping. Our group immediately put their hands down. Except Angie. Gradually those behind stopped clapping as well. Lydia groaned with each strike of Johnny's whip.

Johnny's arm seemed to tire.

"Harder," wheezed Lydia.

"Harder!" demanded Underhill.

"Harder!" we all chanted. "Harder! *Harder!*"

Johnny found his second wind. A loud *thwack* silenced us. Lydia looked shocked. Another loud thwack, and another and she began to float once more.

"Harder," breathed Angie. "I want to feel what she's feeling."

I pinched harder on her nipple and gave it a twist. She groaned. Her hand went up and over the tip of my cock. Underhill's eyes locked on mine. I managed to stifle my moan.

Underhill stepped forward and stood facing Johnny's left side, away from his whip hand. "Make sure the whip goes all the way around." His voice was loud, commanding.

"No, please," whimpered Lydia.

"Sir?" said Johnny.

"All—the—way—around," said Underhill.

Lydia shut her eyes, steeling herself.

Johnny's whip connected around the side of the blonde's body and we saw the tips of the whip strike her.

"Further," said Underhill.

Johnny wasn't hitting her as hard, but now the whip was striking the side of Lydia's breast."

"Harder," demanded Underhill.

Lydia bit her lip. Johnny's whip began to leave thin pink stripes on her breast.

"All—the—way—around," said Underhill.

The strands of the whip wrapped further and further around, leaving red streaks on Lydia's pale white skin. She gasped each time they connected with her nipple. Angie groaned and I gave her nipple an extra-hard pinch. Lydia stared forward, glorying in her ability to absorb the pain, glorying in her ability to transform it into pleasure, glorying in the spell she was weaving over all of us. Sweat splashed up every time the whip connected.

"Is she hot?" asks Underhill.

Johnny transferred the whip to his left hand and laid his right on Lydia's back. "Very hot."

"Is she wet?"

"Yes, Sir. She's sweat—"

"That I can see with my own eyes. Is she wet?"

Johnny gulped and put his hand between Lydia's legs. We could see his fingers pop out through her pubic hair, then disappear. "Yes, sir. Definitely wet."

Underhill motioned towards Lydia's legs and Johnny began whipping them. The cat-o-nine-tails circled around each leg, leaving red streaks behind. Angie slid her hand up and down my penis, giving it a light squeeze each time the whip connected.

"Higher," demanded Underhill. "Make sure the whip gets wet too."

Johnny altered the direction of his strikes and now his arm, and the whip, swung higher. The strands of leather snaked upward, momentarily covering Lydia's pubic hair. She took deep breaths, but Johnny wasn't striking hard.

Angie took my hand out from under her blouse and put it up her dress. Her panties were soaked. "I want to feel what Lydia is feeling."

"Harder!" demanded Underhill.

"Harder," whispered Angie.

I gave her panties a light tap.

The whip slapped against Lydia's genitals. "Ow!" she cried.

"Harder!"

"Harder!" said Angie. "Make it as hard on mine as it is on hers."

Johnny's whip slapped upwards. I gave Angie a firm tap. Both women moaned. Slap. Tap. Moans. Slap. Tap. Moans. Johnny struck harder. I tapped so hard my fingers pressed Angie's panties deep inside. Both women groaned their appreciation.

Lydia was floating again, even as the whip punished her genitals. I kept my taps in time with Johnny's strikes, altering their intensity to aim between eliciting a moan or a groan from Angie.

Underhill clapped his hands. Johnny stopped. "Use the handle," Underhill told him. "In and out. Make the bitch come."

As Johnny altered his position to comply, Angie whispered into my ear, "I want you to think about fucking her."

Lydia's eyes bugged out as she strained to accommodate the whip handle.

"I'd rather be making love to you," I whispered back.

Angie looked at me quizzically, then gave my cock a hard squeeze. "Today I want you to think about Lydia." My eyes were still on her. She gave my cock another squeeze. "Watch *Lydia*!"

Lydia was wiggling her torso back and forth, her direction opposite to the back and forth strokes Johnny was employing with the whip handle. When Johnny began to move the leather handle in and out, she stood still to fully appreciate the sensations.

Johnny used his other hand on the front of Lydia's body, pulling up on her vulva.

Lydia rocked her hips forward. "Harder! Faster!" she urged.

Johnny did his best to comply. His motions were chaotic. But Lydia's were straight back and forth.

"Fuck her!" urged Angie.

"Yes!" I groaned.

"What does it feel like?"

"Hot and wet."

"Fuck her *harder*!"

"Fuck!"

Lydia's skin flushed. Now she was pink everywhere. She stared straight into Underhill's eyes. Her hips rocked back and forth faster and faster. Johnny almost lost his grip on the whip. Lydia rocked faster, faster and harder—

Angie bent over and enveloped my pole with her mouth. I couldn't help but look down. I know she wanted me to watch Lydia but the whole universe had collapsed into her brunette curls bobbing up and down.

Lydia screamed and finally I was able to look up at her. I fucked her then—hard and fast and mercilessly. We both came at the exact same moment. The crowd swallowed her gasping spasms. Angie swallowed my pumping passion. But my last spurt, I saved for Lydia.

Back in my room, I locked my door, flipped the mechanical door security bar and set the chair up against the door lever. Then I inserted Jackie's memory key into the slot on the side of my laptop.

The memory key took forever to load. My mind roared, impatient to know what Jackie had extracted from Underhill's computer.

Finally it had loaded. But all I could see were file folders and a partial list of the documents inside each. None of the documents would open. And judging from the nonsensical names of the folders and files, even these had been encrypted.

I transferred the files through my phone and uploaded the entire contents of the memory key into the cloud. I made sure no traces had been left on my laptop. Then I slipped the memory key under the bed mattress.

Using my cellphone, I carefully composed an oblique email to my friend, the former R.C.M.P. officer, asking for his help to decrypt what I'd just uploaded. I pressed 'send', replaced the cellphone in the safe, and headed for the washroom.

After a long and hard shower, I took the cellphone out of the safe. My friend had responded! My heart began to race. But I sighed as I read his message, "Sorry, old buddy, we can't break the encryption. Maybe Antoine Jonquiére in Montreal or the Americans could, but I don't have the pull to test those waters any more. One of the downsides of retirement. But I can tell you that the contents of the files are extensive and likely include images as well as text."

Antoine in Montreal—that was a bridge I'd burned long ago. The only thing he hated more than me was the way the F.B.I. treated him.

I started to smack the mirror but pulled my hand up short. Damn! As usual, my long shot was a bust. Jackie, or whatever her name was, was likely part of Underhill's competition. She knew I had the memory key. Who knew what her next move would be, but it wouldn't be good! Would somebody be sent to kill me, mount a more direct assault on Underhill's operation? Not for the first time, I wished I knew more about Jackie Warne.

My phone beeped. A reminder of next week's disciplinary meeting and the impending implosion of my career. I shook my head. My personal life was in shambles too. The only sex I was getting was from a woman who was doing it to please her boss. My motives, to turn her into an asset, were even less romantic.

I felt my shoulders slump. After what seemed forever, I wiped the most recent transactions from the cellphone and replaced it in the safe. I tried to take a deep breath, but there was a heaviness in my chest. I was momentarily grateful that there wasn't a personal service weapon in the safe.

Somehow, my back ended up on the mattress. I stared up at the mirror on the ceiling, unable to sleep.

Chapter 9 *Jackie*

I lay on my bed, very still, concentrating on keeping my breathing steady. It was the middle of the night. But something was wrong; something had woken me up. My breathing was steady, but my heart was racing a mile-a-minute.

Finally—forever!—my eyes adjusted to the darkness. Someone was sitting next to my bed. I couldn't hear his breathing. Maybe he'd fallen asleep. Maybe he was just a perv, sneaking into my room. I started to inch towards the other side of the bed.

"Good morning," he said, his voice deep, masculine, and somehow familiar.

I turned towards him. Pervs were best confronted head on. "What do you want?" I tried to calculate how best to kick him squarely in the balls.

He held up his hand. Something glinted at the top of his fingers. "Interesting things inside this. How did you crack his computer so fast?"

"Whose computer?" I asked, then corrected myself. "Who said I cracked anybody's computer?" It wasn't a perv; it was Kyle Fairbairn, Underhill's security chief.

He waved the memory key back and forth. "This little flash drive says so." Light momentarily flashed across his teeth as he held it closer. "You remember this, don't you? The one you put into Mr. Underhill's computer. The one I took out of the cute little pouch in your pants?"

I quickly calculated the distance to my nightstand. I was closer and he was off to the side. I took a deep breath and lunged for the drawer handle. There was something on my ankles, but I managed to yank the drawer open. Except it was empty!?!

Kyle held up my sidearm. "Looking for this?"

Shit! He's got my gun. I dove towards the other side of the bed. But now something cinched tightly around my ankles.

"Tsk, tsk," he tutted. "Something got your feet?"

I tried to reach for my feet, but he pressed my sidearm against my shoulder. I could probably take him, but the gun would make it dangerous. I flopped back down onto the mattress and exhaled loudly so that he'd think he'd defeated me. It didn't help that I'd been hot when I'd gone to bed. I was nude. The bastard had probably enjoyed looking up my legs. I didn't know how I was going to get out of this, but I did know that I should have turned him into Underhill when I'd had the chance.

He popped the magazine out of the pistol butt and ejected the round from the chamber. He pocketed the magazine and the bullet, but laid the gun on the nightstand. Why would he?!? But I didn't have time to think about that. I readied a fist strike to his throat. Except that he sat back in his chair.

"Now Jackie, or whatever your name is, I have about ten minutes before I'm missed. In those ten minutes, you're going to tell me what you're up to. If you don't, I'm going to tell Underhill that I discovered that you're with the Russian mob and that you're trying to infiltrate his crew. The proof is already on your computer." He tapped my sidearm. "An illegal weapon is just icing on the cake."

"How far the R.C.M.P. have fallen."

"R.C.M.P.?"

"Kyle, oh by the way your real name is Keith Martin, and you're a dishonorably discharged Royal Canadian Mounted Police Officer."

"How do you know I'm with the R.C.M.P.?"

"More like used to be. Your temporary suspension will be permanent after your superiors find out that you've been paying off Jamaican politicians."

He looked at his watch. "Nine minutes."

"Nine minutes and you're going to turn me in? Really! And how do you propose to explain how you got ahold of the flash drive?"

"I'm not going to say *anything* about the flash drive. It's evidence. And if *you* mention the flash drive, Underhill will know that you're a spy."

"A spy?"

"Trying to take over Underhill's operation for yourself. You're as bad as he is."

Well, at least Kyle/Keith didn't know that I'm with the F.B.I. "How did you get ahold of my computer?"

"Standard search procedure."

"That you learned from the Mounties."

He looked at his watch again. "Seven minutes."

"What did you find on the flash drive?"

He hesitated. He couldn't break the encryption!

"That's not your concern," he said. "Your concern is to tell me precisely who you are, who's behind you, and what you're up to." He looked at his watch. "Five minutes."

"Your concern is—"

"Let me worry about my concerns—"

"Of which there are many." And one more. I'd managed to work my right foot free of the rope he'd snared it with.

"Your concern is whether Underhill kills you. If you want to avoid that fate, you'd better tell me who you are, who you're working for and what you're up to."

"So you're not an R.C.M.P. Officer—"

"Who I am is not your concern."

"If you're not an R.C.M.P. Officer, how can I trust you not to turn me in to Underhill?"

"You don't have a choice."

"And, you don't have the foggiest idea what's on the flash drive."

"Whether I do or not is not your concern. Four minutes."

"I need to know what's on the flash drive."

"You need—"

"The question is, do *you* need to know what's on the flash drive?"

He looked at me. Defeated? "You're right, I do need to know what's on the flash drive."

"Why?"

"To put human traffickers, like you, like Underhill, out of business. Three minutes."

"What do you care? You're just in it for the money?"

"You would know."

"I would know. I read your file, remember? Or rather I read Keith Martin's file."

"That file is classified."

"Not to me."

"Who *are* you?"

I heard feet in the distance. Underhill was going to be here any minute. I had to take a chance on Keith Martin. I had no other play. Even though I'd worked my second foot free, we'd still be in the middle of a fist-fight when Underhill arrived. Keith didn't turn me in when he found the flash drive. Still. Shit!

"Two minutes."

"My name is Special Agent Jennifer Logan. With the F.B.I."

I watched Martin's face.

His eyes went as wide as saucers.

"We can work together," I told him. "You haven't been able to get inside my flash drive, have you?"

He slowly shook his head.

Feet sounded loudly on the stairs leading up to my room.

"That's Underhill," he said, stating the obvious.

"I hope you locked the door behind you."

"He has a pass key."

"For the whole resort?"

Martin nodded. "We have to have sex."

"I beg your pardon?!?"

"If we're not having sex, how do you explain us being together in your room in the middle of the night?"

"Use the latch key."

"We have to come out sooner or later. Kyle and Jackie have to have sex!"

There was a loud knock at the door. Then Joel's voice: "Miss Warne, have you seen Kyle?"

"Who I do or do not see is none of your business," I yelled.

"Whom," whispered Martin.

I shot him a dirty look.

Joel banged the door again. "Let's see what happens when it's Mr. Underhill doing the asking." His feet stomped off.

I got up and flipped the latchkey to physically lock the door. Before I remembered that I was nude. Martin was momentarily startled. At how round my bum was, or the fact that my ankles were no longer tied? He looked at my body, then at the loose bindings on the bed. When he looked back up to me, I bounced back atop the bed and told him: "You have to leave."

He shook his head. "So you can turn me into Underhill?"

"I told you, I'm F.B.I.—"

"All the more reason to turn me in. The F.B.I. gets all the credit."

I scowled at him and pulled the sheets up to my neck. His concern wasn't without basis. "You'd better tell me everything about why you're here."

"I haven't been a good boy back home. I'm a clean cop, but I've stepped on some toes. I'm up on disciplinary charges. No one from the R.C.M.P. knows I'm down here. If I can snag Underhill, the planet will be a better place and I can leave the force with my head held high."

"Or maybe they'll reinstate you."

"That would be nice, but I wouldn't count on it. Even if we do snag Underhill."

"We?"

"We. I have the flash drive, remember?"

Steps sound at the bottom of the stairs. They could still be Joel's.

Kyle stood and removed his shirt. "We have to have sex," he repeated. He stepped to the door and opened the security latch. "If Underhill can't get in, it'll only make matters worse. He'll be livid!" When he came back to the bed, I let him pull my sheet down, but only as far as my belly.

The steps on the stairs paused. Kyle removed his pants and briefs all in one jerky motion. He was already starting to get erect. My breasts might be pushing fifty, but at least they still had that effect!

He tugged on the sheet. "Jackie and Kyle have to have sex."

"There must be another way—" The feet on the stairs were moving. And there were voices.

"We have to have sex." The steps were nearing the top of the stairs. Kyle's voice was desperate. The voices on the stairs were louder. One was male.

There had to be another way. But damn if I could think of what it might be! It didn't help my thought processes that Kyle, a big, muscular and very sexy man was standing inches away from me. My pussy certainly liked the idea of Jackie and Kyle having sex. And she was interfering with my higher cognitive functions.

Kyle was fully erect. Unlike Underhill, he wasn't huge. But his cock was certainly throbbing with desire! I wasn't sure that I wanted to have sex with Kyle. Underhill was just the target of an investigation; there was a thrill in using my feminine wiles to snare him. Sex with a target wouldn't lead to emotional entanglements after the fact. But Kyle was a fellow police officer. Outside the door, one set of feet touched the landing at the top of the stairs. The male voice below was definitely Underhill's.

I let Kyle pull my sheet to the bottom of the bed. His eyes bulged as my legs slowly spread outwards.

He jumped right on top of me and I braced for a savage

onslaught. But Kyle was completely gentle. Like a warm and cuddly teddy bear. He supported his weight almost entirely with his arms and knees. Only our bellies and hips touched. His cock was warm on my legs. I could feel his heartbeat on my thighs.

Kyle's lips softly kissed my cheek. His sweat was a heady mix of fear, desperation and bravado. He moved to kiss my other cheek. But I wanted more and kissed him fully on the mouth. His cock pressed at the opening to my pussy. I could immediately tell that she was wet, eager to be penetrated.

"Please," I begged.

"Are you sure?"

My answer was a deep moan.

He pushed himself forward but just the tip of his cock entered my pussy. I responded with a sharp upward thrust of my hips and he slid half way up inside. The forces of nature rocked his hips in the other direction and our pubic bones pressed together. He was warm. The length of our bodies slid up and down against each other. I could tell that he was soft in some places, hard in others, but in the moment I wasn't aware of which was which. Somehow our bodies just fit together perfectly. Somehow having sex with Kyle just seemed *right*!

Sex with Underhill had been pure carnality. Kyle was less intense, but there was a real tenderness in him. With Bernie, our bodies *connected*; Kyle's connection was less forceful, but somehow deeper, more dynamic.

I relaxed into Kyle's gently rhythm, like floating on the waves of the ocean, calming, protected. But today, the ocean was being naughty and her waves were lapping with extra force up my legs and into my—

A knock sounded at the door. Kyle's rhythmic thrusts brought me back into the cocoon he was weaving around us.

Kyle started pumping more forcefully. He felt grand. Grand?!? What was I, a teenager!? His weight on my hips meant that I could only move an inch or two, but my twitchings seemed to inspire him to ever-faster thrusts. Nonetheless, at the end of each stroke, he paused to caress our pubic bones together. And every time he did so, little sparks danced around inside my pussy and up my spine.

There was a rustling outside my door. Then the palm of a hand slammed against the door. "Kyle!" bellowed Underhill.

Kyle started to pull himself up and off me. "Don't you dare," I told him. I lifted myself upwards, grabbed his hips and rocked him back inside me.

"But—"

"But shit! Finish what you started!" I relaxed downward against the mattress and he slid half way out.

He hesitated.

"Please!"

Kyle nodded, his mind made up. He slammed his cock into me and I gasped. Before I could take another breath, he'd wrenched himself out of me and crashed his entire weight against me. Thankfully after three sharp strokes, he lifted himself up by his arms. But that was only to allow him to more furiously plunge himself in and out of me and I could only gasp little gulps of air into my lungs.

Bang! The door rattled on his hinges. "Kyle!" Underhill sounded furious.

Kyle paused, just long enough for me to fill my lungs. When he started his ferocious assault up again, I was able to rock my hips just enough to make his pubic bone pull up on my clit. Every time he caressed her, I inched closer and closer to climax.

Bang! The door sounded as if it was about to splinter into a thousand pieces. "Kyle!"

But now Kyle seemed oblivious to anything but me. His teeth gritted with his exertions. But his eyes possessed me, worshiped me with fervent devotion, as if I was the only thing in all creation.

My pussy was warm and wet and tight. Every time Kyle plunged his cock into me, she became tighter and tighter, wrapped in bands of sparking electricity. Little jolts escaped as the bands squeezed tighter and tighter. He plunged in and when he pulled back out, he sucked all the air out of my lungs.

Hands clapped in the distance.

"Arrrghh!" screamed Kyle.

The bands burst inside me! "Kyle!" I screamed. His cock pounded lightning up my spine. Wave after wave! Then he was slipping and sliding and I couldn't feel as much. But it was warm and wonderful. I reached up to hug him, to pull his lips to mine.

The clapping hands came closer. "Bravo!" It was Underhill's voice. We broke off the kiss and looked sideways into Bernie's smiling face. "Bravo! Bravo!" he beamed.

Kyle slid off me and tried to pull the sheet over us. Underhill stepped forward and gave Kyle a light slap across his face. "Well done, my friend. She's a real minx, isn't she?" Bernie blew me a kiss.

Angie poked her head around Bernie's torso. First surprise, then hurt, then resignation flitted across her face. She turned and sped out of the room. Joel looked around at everyone, then he too beat a hasty retreat.

Underhill looked around then shrugged when he realized the three of us were alone. He pointed at Kyle: "In the morning, bright and early in the dining room." Then his finger took both of us within its wave. "Make sure you get some sleep." There was a smirk on his face as he left the room.

Kyle and I collapsed together on the bed, flush with having survived Underhill's foray, flush with sexual afterglow. Kyle hadn't repeatedly taken me over the edge of abyss the way Bernie had, but somehow I felt more contented. I gave his thigh a gentle squeeze.

We lay together for some time, breathing together. Then I crawled off the bed, enjoying his eyes fondling my body. I booted up my laptop and held out my hand for the memory key.

"How do I know I can trust you?" he asked.

"How do I know I can trust *you*?" I shot back.

"Because—"

"Because—"

"—I didn't turn you in to Underhill," we both finished in unison. We both wanted to laugh, but neither dared.

Kyle slowly fished the flash drive out of his pants pocket and then made a show of being reluctant to hand it over.

As soon as I popped the memory key into my computer, an icon appeared on the desktop. When I clicked on it, a series of files and folders displayed themselves in a running list. But, like Kyle, I was unable to open any of the documents.

I opened my internet cloud application. "I'll have to send them to Washington for decryption."

"Why you?"

"Because *you* can't."

"You have to tell them that it's a joint R.C.M.P. – F.B.I. operation."

"If I do, my superiors will have to notify Toronto."

"Ottawa."

"Ottawa, I stand corrected." Ottawa was Canada's capital, where the R.C.M.P. was headquartered. Kyle was pulling his clothes back on.

I started to compose the email—"But wait. No one in Ottawa knows you're here?"

He slumped back to the bed. "And reporting it to Ottawa will involve too many people."

"Who knows where Underhill has eyes and ears."

He nodded and made a vague wave in the direction of my computer. I was to send everything to Washington, and Washington only.

As the files started uploading to the cloud, I turned back to Kyle. He still looked glum. I pointed to the bed. "That was nice," I told him.

His eyes followed my finger to the scattered sheets atop the bed. "Nice?"

"Having sex with you. It was nice."

He smiled and nodded. "Yes, it was. Nice."

"A pleasant perk of the job."

"Just the job?" He looked glum again. Hurt?

"Well...that's how we met."

"But you didn't have to."

I glanced at the files being uploaded to the cloud. Actually, he was wrong about that; we hadn't had a choice. But I smiled, "No, we didn't have to."

He shot me a sharp look. Shit—he was a *trained* investigator. And he had caught me in a lie.

I pretended to pout. "Well, we didn't have to *enjoy* it."

That seemed to cheer him up a bit.

I leaned over and patted his hand. "And I really, really enjoyed it!"

He nodded, a half smile returning to his lips. There was an awkward moment. He got up and went to the door. As he opened it, I took his hand and pulled him down to me. He kissed my cheek. I kissed him on the lips. Our tongues touched, then withdrew, frightened, back into the depths of our mouths.

He smiled and I suddenly remembered that I was still nude. I hid behind the door and waved good-bye. First his feet, then his torso, then his shoulders disappeared behind the railing. Finally his head.

And then he was gone. For the first time in a long time I felt alone. I was full of longing, but also flush with anticipation. First Bernie. Then Kyle! What was getting into me?!? I had a job to do.

I sat down at my computer and typed out a detailed report, leaving out everything between my kisses with Kyle. Buried in the last paragraph was a note that an additional day would be required. I pressed 'send', then quickly checked my inbox, hoping against hope that they'd decrypted the files I'd just uploaded. But my inbox was empty. As empty as my heart.

I got up to go to the washroom, but the disarray of sheets on my bed caught my eye. Had I just had sex with Kyle Fairbairn? Or Keith Martin? Or…? With Bernie sex had been feral and powerful and physical. Very powerful! Sex with Kyle had been nice, but it had had an additional dimension. Tenderness surely. Even affection.

Chapter 10 *Kyle*

Four hours later, I awoke light-headed and giddy. Shaving almost made me laugh. It took all my willpower to bang out the latest installment in my 'novel'. I only thought about Jackie once or twice. Okay, maybe twenty times. In my head, I knew last night was only business. Still, I was having a hard time getting Jackie, or rather Jennifer Logan, out of my mind.

I called Antoine Jonquiére at the Force's Montreal detachment. He hated my guts. But even more, he hated the F.B.I. always taking credit for the R.C.M.P.'s hard work. Hopefully the Americans had ticked him off recently. "The F.B.I. is trying to screw us over," I told him which got his attention long enough for me to explain the situation.

"I know da guy in Interpol," he said. "I'm booking the *vacance* in Montego Bay. If you get evidence on Underhill, the Force *rembourse* the expense. Udderwise, you pay."

"Done," I told him.

In the dining room, Underhill was in fine fettle, exulting in how blue was the sky, how warm was the sun and how sweet was the pineapple. "I have decided," he said, then paused for everyone to wait on tenterhooks for his announcement. "I have decided that tonight we will have an orgy in the Romping Room." There was scattered applause, especially from Joel and Johnny. I maintained professional non-committal. Jackie hadn't clapped. "Meanwhile," continued Underhill, "enjoy the resort, and have a nap. Mr. Ritchie and I have business to attend to."

After his entourage had returned to their breakfasts, Underhill waved me over. "Joel and I are going into Montego Bay. Our rental car will be arriving shortly. Book the Romping Room for the party."

We all saw Underhill off an hour later. I made a show of inspecting the rental car, a black Toyota Camry, and giving it a once-over with Johnny's security wand. Joel put his laptop in the back seat. He adjusted the headrest then tapped his fingers on the steering wheel as all the women kissed Underhill goodbye. Shaneese was the last one in line and she lingered over her kiss as she rubbed her body up and down Underhill's. That made the other women want to come back for seconds. Joel sighed and rested his forehead on the steering wheel.

Underhill caught me looking at Jackie. He waved me over, angled his head towards her and grabbed my shoulder. "Make sure you take a nap!" he teased. "You'll need *all* your energies tonight!"

I nodded, embarrassed at being caught, and waited for him to release my shoulder. I prayed Jackie hadn't noticed.

Everyone else turned back inside the resort as soon as Underhill's car was halfway down the driveway. Jackie and I watched his departure with more than a little trepidation.

"Do you think he's coming back?" she asked.

"There's no way to tell. Any news on the contents of the flash drive?"

She shook her head. "I'm going to rent a car; if they take off again, I want to be ready."

"If they come back."

"If they come back."

At that moment her phone rang. She scowled at the screen. "My boss," she said. She swiped right and took the call. She walked away, arguing, so I went into the lobby to book the space for Underhill's latest orgy.

Despite my pleas for an early start time, I couldn't book the Romping Room until 3 a.m., its usual closing time.

As I turned from the reception clerk, Jackie was suddenly there, a look of satisfaction on her face. "A grey Honda Civic will arrive this afternoon."

We agreed to go to our separate rooms and get as much shut-eye as possible. Underhill would nap in the car. We needed to be as fresh as possible. Jackie kissed me at my door, then left.

I flopped my back onto the mattress, looked up at the ceiling mirror and gave it a kiss. I shut my eyes and kissed Jackie over and over again. She kissed me back, then gave me a soft shove sending me floating downward into darkness.

Only when I woke up did I remember that we'd been worried that Underhill wouldn't come back. Bugging out when the authorities had been getting close was one of the reasons he'd never been brought to justice. Two years ago, the cops had been coming in one door while he was escaping out the other.

However, Underhill and Joel arrived back in time for dinner, looking refreshed and excited. Johnny hustled off to get food for the boss.

Nara leaned in to whisper in Joel's ear. I didn't hear what she'd said, but his response was, "Everything's in place, the final details should lock in tonight."

After the main course, Underhill raised his glass in my direction, "Tonight, the Romping Room!"

I shook my head and he lowered his glass. "I'm sorry, Mr. Underhill, I could only book it for after three a.m."

His face clouded as he considered my news. He turned to Joel. "Will that work?"

Joel typed into his computer. I leaned towards Underhill. "If you have business, we can postpone the orgy."

He shook his head. "Nonsense! The whole point of business is the pleasures it brings." He waved his arm around the table, taking us all in, and the resort beyond.

Everyone fell silent and watched Joel type. Finally Underhill's assistant nodded.

Underhill's smile returned and once more he raised his glass in my direction. "We'll play nines in the Romping Room at three!"

Everyone clapped. A glance from Underhill sent Johnny scurrying for dessert.

I leaned over to Angie. "What does he mean 'we'll play nines'?"

"It's a card game. Each player has a card. Since there are nine of us, we'll play with the Ace and the number cards up to nine. The tens and the face cards will be discarded."

"Underhill's the ace."

She nodded as if it was the stupidest question possible. "Everyone draws a card. If you draw your card, you get to pick two people to act out a dare. If two or more people each get their card, all of them have to act out something."

"Sounds complicated."

She shrugged. "Bernie deals with any contingencies."

After dinner, everyone dispersed to get a nap. I hung around afterwards and was pleased to see that Jackie had been slow to leave as well. "Why do you think he wants us all together for a sexfest in the midst of his deal?" she asked.

"Maybe he's worried he has a mole."

"Or more than one mole." She gave me a peck on the cheek and headed towards her room. "Time for another nap," she said over her shoulder.

Between the nap I'd had earlier, thinking about Jackie, and

worrying about Underhill's pending transaction, all I could do was stare up into the mirror above my bed.

Finally, it was three a.m.

In the Romping Room, Underhill gathered us in a circle around the mattresses. Everyone was dressed in Jamaican colors, tonight's theme. Jackie was wearing a green, gold and black bikini. Angie had a form-fitting dress with horizontal bands of green, gold, black, white and red. Lydia and Shaneese were wearing green bustiers and yellow hot pants. Nara had a two-piece silk outfit which draped elegantly over her slender figure. The top was black, the bottom green. I, and the rest of the men, were wearing shirts and shorts.

Joel had his laptop propped in a chair, but its screen was facing away from the circle. He entered a few keystrokes then joined us.

Underhill picked up the deck from which Johnny had already removed the surplus cards and dealt one card to each of us.

The only one who got her card was Nara. She looked around at all of us, a smile spreading on her face as she considered each possible dare. Finally she motioned Johnny and Shaneese into the centre of the circle. Nara pointed to Johnny, "Tell Shaneese what you'd like her to do with her right hand. But you can only give her general instructions such as up and down, forward and back. As soon as she touches you, you have to close your eyes."

Johnny nodded. "Forward."

Shaneese rested her hand on his shoulder. He shut his eyes. "Sideways."

She quickly moved her hand to the center of his chest. "Down. But slowly."

The black hand moved down to his belly but angled to his right. When the hand moved below his belly button, it was obvious it was going to go down his right leg.

"Left," he told her.

But Shaneese went to *her* left and missed his genitals altogether.

"Right! Right!"

She moved her hand between his legs, continuing downward. "Up!"

Shaneese started upward, but angling to his left. "A little left."

Shaneese went way left. Everyone burst out laughing.

"Be a good girl," Underhill told her.

She came back to the center, touching the front of Johnny's bright green shorts.

"Stop!" said Johnny. There was a dreamy look on his face. Shaneese held her hand motionless.

"Circles. Make circles."

Shaneese made slow circles with her hand. Johnny was in seventh heaven. A bulge grew under his shorts.

Underhill clapped his hands. "Bravo!"

Shaneese withdrew her hand. Johnny opened his eyes, clearly disappointed.

Underhill dealt the cards again.

Underhill got an Ace. He motioned Nara into the center of the circle. "Hard or soft?" he asked her.

"Hard."

Underhill smiled. "Remove your top."

Nara lifted her top over her head. She wasn't wearing a bra. Her breasts were small and perfectly proportioned, her nipples little dark spots. If anything, she looked more elegant than before.

"Shut your eyes," he told her. When she'd complied, Underhill continued, "Everyone line up. Pinch her nipples once, then move on. The second time you pinch, pinch harder. You'll keep pinching until she guesses the culprit."

I was last in line. Underhill went first. Nara gasped or moaned as her nipples were being pinched. Obviously different people had different techniques. Joel, who was immediately in front of me, cupped her entire breasts before taking her nipples between his fingers and gently rotating. Her eyes flickered open as she moaned and it was obvious she'd recognized Joel. A sharp look from her dark brown eyes told me to keep my mouth shut. Joel pulled his fingers downward and she gasped.

Nara's breasts were soft, warm and smooth. Or at least the parts directly around her nipples were. I didn't dare take as many liberties as Joel had. Her nipples were small, but very hard. As soon as I had them between my thumbs and forefingers, she whispered, "Hard."

I gave them a hard twist.

"Aiee!" she yelped.

Nara yelped even louder when Underhill took his second

turn. This time through, her gasps were shorter and sharper. Moans were replaced with groans. Ahead of me, Joel went straight for her nipples and twisted. She kept her eyes shut and sucked her lower lip into her mouth, holding her breath. He twisted harder. She bit her lip and scrunched her eyes. He twisted harder. She gasped. He twisted— "Joel!" she yelled.

Underhill clapped and we all joined in.

A beep from the laptop sent Joel and Underhill scurrying over to it. The rest of us broke up into little groups.

I managed to sidle up next to Jackie and whisper into her ear, "Something is definitely going down. We should call in the cavalry and arrest them." She was soft and warm.

Jackie shook her head. "It's too early for me to call in the back-up. We have to let the transaction develop if we want to take down the whole network."

"It's something big."

"Maybe. Or just one valuable item."

"They could be smuggling human beings."

"Kyle—"

"Children."

"Even so. If we move too quickly, the network will simply cut Underhill out and carry on as before."

"Jackie—"

But at that moment, Underhill picked up the remaining cards and dealt them. He got an ace and all the women got their cards as well. "Okay," he said. "Last time it was Nara's turn to be the centre of attention, this time, me. I will shut my eyes and put my hands behind my head. Each of you," he said, pausing to point at the women, "will do what you do and the first one I guess will win a prize. No touching above the neck."

The women swarmed around Underhill and swiftly had him standing nude. Nude but flaccid. Then they lined up single file. Shaneese softly scratched her nails down his back. Nara made little pinches down his spine. Angie started from the top and caressed the spots they'd touched. Lydia twisted his nipples. Jackie kissed a random pattern up his spine. Underhill smiled throughout but had no other reaction.

If Jackie had kissed me like that, I'd be doing more than smiling.

Shaneese stepped forward for round two and gently raked her

fingernails up his buttocks. I squirmed on my seat. Nara pinched the underside of his bottom. Angie caressed it all over. Lydia pinched skin just below his balls and twisted. Jackie started at the upper right of his right buttock then kissed at an angle down to the lower left buttock. At the end, she seemed to blow. I shivered, imagining Jackie blowing warm air on my body. She kept blowing. Underhill was silent until just before Jackie raised her head. Then he let out a low groan. I had to stifle my own groan.

Shaneese paused, then stepped directly in front of Underhill and rubbed her fingers back and forth across his nipples. Nara gave them a sharp pinch, not letting go until he gasped. Angie lightly kissed Nara's pain away then gently licked each nipple in turn. Lydia twisted his nipples, harder this time. Jackie sucked long and sensuously on his right nipple. I felt a stirring below my belt, remembering when she'd sucked my nipple. She kissed her mouth over to his left nipple. Underhill smacked his lips. When she sucked her lips up and off his nipple, it was noticeably larger than before. He patted her head.

Shaneese looked back and forth between Underhill's hand and Jackie's head. That *hadn't* been part of the game. I heaved a sigh of relief when the large black woman shrugged and bent down in front of Bernie's balls. She took the longest finger of her right hand and, barely touching, raked it back and forth on the underside of his ball sack. Underhill let out an extended moan, his penis beginning to engorge. Nara gave his balls a gentle upwards swat. He yelped. Angie sucked one of his balls into and out of her mouth. He moaned throughout. Each time a woman touched his balls, Underhill's penis enlarged. Jackie took both balls in her hand and gently caressed them. Underhill said, "Mmmmm," and his penis seemed to grow each time her fingers moved.

Shaneese pulled Jackie away, knelt in front of Underhill, and gently ran her tongue up and down his erection. Then she sucked the head of his penis into her mouth, forcing him to gasp shallow breaths into his lungs. He exhaled and took a deep breath when she stood.

Jackie was still standing where Shaneese had pulled her. Our eyes met. There was hunger there.

Next in kneeling position was Nara. She plunged her mouth halfway down his cock and sucked. Her fingers dug into his butt.

"Nara!" screamed Underhill. He opened his eyes and looked down at her, his eyes speaking equal measures of admiration and rebuke.

"I didn't get a chance!" protested Angie and Lydia in unison.

Underhill brought Angie and Lydia together in a hug.

Jackie glanced over at me. What was she thinking? What would she have done if Underhill hadn't guessed whose fingernails were digging into his bum?

Joel and Underhill huddled over the laptop. Everyone went over to the largest of the three pools and dipped their feet in. I unlocked the door and stepped outside, making a show of fulfilling my security obligations.

When I re-entered and locked the door behind me, Underhill and his assistant were still staring into the laptop. Jackie was off to the side of the group. She glanced towards the two men huddled over the laptop, then back to me. I wished this wasn't work. I wished I could take her away and walk along the beach, holding hands, listening to the ocean.

Jackie glanced back to Joel and Underhill. Maybe here is where she'd rather be.

Underhill suddenly stood upright and clapped his hands. Something good was obviously happening. Good for—

Underhill strode to the centre of the mattresses. Everyone else scrambled to re-establish the circle. I ended up to the left of Joel. Jackie was just to his right, so I couldn't see her.

Underhill picked up the cards and shuffled. He seemed to fumble with them. Then he dealt. Angie, Jackie and I each got our cards. Underhill rubbed his hands together. "It's time for Ring Around the Rosie," he decreed.

Angie stepped forward and pulled Jackie and I into the centre of the circle as Underhill stepped aside, taking the cards with him. "What're we supposed to do?" I asked her. Jackie looked as confused as I was.

"Ring Around the Rosie is threesome where two of us take turns pleasuring the person at the centre."

"Ring around the Rosie," Underhill began in a sing-song, "Pocket full of posies, Angie, Jackie, Kyle? This time it's Angie!"

Angie, the only one of us who'd apparently played the game before, stepped between us. When Jackie and I just looked at her, she whispered, "Touch me."

Angie's multi-colored dress hugged her body, so it was easy for Jackie to move behind Angie and touch the middle of her back. I moved in front and caressed her tummy. The dress was made of cotton, very thin cotton. Angie was soft and warm.

"Up and down," she told us.

I felt Jackie's hands move to Angie's bum. I chose the lesser of two evils and gently danced my fingers up to her breasts.

Angie moaned, then stepped forward into me, rubbing her body up and down mine. She moaned again and I had to stifle my own moan. However, I couldn't stifle the reaction below my belt. I had no choice but to give her breasts a gentle squeeze and she moaned again.

I felt Jackie step forward into Angie, pressing the brunette even more firmly against me. Angie's hips targeted my growing tumescence and this time a groan escaped my lips.

"Ring around the Rosie," began Underhill. This time everyone joined in the sing-song, "Pocket full of posies, Angie, Jackie, Kyle?"

We stepped back from Angie. Her face was flushed, smiling. Two little buds in the centre of her breasts were clearly visible through the thin material of her dress.

Underhill's voice alone completed the ditty, "This time it's Kyle!"

Angie pulled me in between herself and Jackie. Suddenly there were two hands vying to undo my shorts. Their competition was a bit on the intense side and I winced. Mercifully, they found my zipper and my shorts slipped to the floor.

The hands became gentler, but this led to a new problem. I was becoming fully erect and my briefs didn't have enough stretch to accommodate this new development. Hands reached for my tee shirt and pulled it up and over my head. Now the hands were contending for my nipples. In quick order Jackie's fingers caressed my right nipple while Angie's retreated to my left.

"Who's better?" asked Angie.

I looked forward between the two women, shut my eyes, and moaned. There was absolutely no right answer to Angie's question.

The hands left my nipples and once again attacked my gonads. I winced and tried to turn away, but there was no escape.

"Ring around the Rosie," said Underhill, but this time it was a command, not a song.

Angie moved around to my back which allowed Jackie to take my front. Her soft skin, only partially covered by her bikini, was wonderful against mine. But then Angie pushed her aside. I was apparently 'the Rosie' around which the two women were to ring around. Angie's fingers pulled my penis even tighter against my briefs. It hurt, but it wouldn't take much more to make me come.

Jackie pushed her aside and mercifully kissed my lips instead of caressing below.

"Ring around the Rosie, Pocket full of posies, Angie, Jackie, Kyle? This time it's Angie!" And this time, except for the first and last words, everybody joined in the song.

Jackie and I lifted Angie's dress up and off over her head. Angie wiggled with delight. She had no bra. We each fondled a nipple. Her right one was warm and hard. She moaned repeatedly but it was impossible to tell whose fingers were responsible.

Jackie's eyes met mine and I suddenly wished that I was caressing her nipple, not Angie's. Jackie's eyes seemed to echo my desire. Below, my penis yearned to escape the clutches of my brief.

A flicker in our eyes indicated we should go lower. At Angie's belly button, my finger touched Jackie's. It was just for an instant, but I felt it all the way up to my shoulder blades. Angie's belly rippled as our fingers danced lower.

Our fingers met again at the top of Angie's panties. The material was soft, smooth, stretchy and incredibly thin. Angie's heat radiated right through. Jackie's eyes locked into mine. An invisible force dragged our fingers lower and lower until we felt the heat and female juices bubbling out of Angie's vagina.

Our hands moved together to the top of Angie's panties, then slid under. As we moved towards her pubic hair her panties lifted up, then away, sliding down her legs. Jackie's fingers intertwined with mine as we caressed Angie's clit. Then two fingers, one from each of our hands, slid into Angie's roiling cauldron. Angie groaned and we felt the vibration in our palms.

Our fingers stroked back and forth. Angie's knees wobbled. Jackie and I gripped her bum to steady her. Angie moaned with each stroke, each moan louder, less inhibited than the last. She was on the edge of climax. Just a few more strokes—

"Ring around the Rosie, Pocket full of posies, Angie, Jackie, Kyle? This time it's Jackie!" Someone else had started the song, but, as before, Underhill had had the last word.

Angie shuddered and she climbed down from the edge of her

climax. I had Jackie all to myself and I hugged her to me, planting a firm kiss on her mouth. Her tongue darted inside. Her bikini pressed against my thigh. Her tummy was warm, especially where it rubbed up and down the front of my briefs.

Jackie moaned, breaking off the kiss. I felt fingertips on my balls. Jackie's tummy shuddered. My penis burned with pleasure and pain as it pressed against my brief. A groan opened my eyes. Angie was behind Jackie, caressing back and forth along the bottom of her bikini, her fingers sometimes touching me.

I slid my hands under the top of Jackie's bikini. Her nipples were hard, her breasts warm. Her every breath was a moan or a groan, the fingers above and the fingers below pushing her arousal deeper and deeper.

"Ring around the Rosie," demanded Underhill's voice.

I moved around to Jackie's backside and caressed her bottom. Angie's hands were on Jackie's breasts. I lifted up the bikini. "Suck them," I said.

Angie's hands immediately left one breast, leaving a nipple open for me to play with. Jackie gasped, though more likely from what Angie's mouth was doing, not from my fingers.

I slid a hand down to between Jackie's legs. Her bikini was thin, ever so thin! Her warmth was palpable. And moist where Angie had been touching. A deep groan escaped Jackie's lungs. This time I was pretty sure I could take the credit!

I played with the edges of Jackie's bikini. Should I slip a finger inside? She groaned again which I took as an invitation. Her skin was so soft and my finger pressed against where the elastic in her bikini pressed it deep into her flesh. Then down the front where the material was thinnest. My finger became warmer and warm—

"Ring around the Rosie, Pocket full of posies, Angie, Jackie, Kyle? This time it's Kyle!" I recognized Nara's voice as starting the song. Had she dared join Underhill in choosing my name?

The two women quickly stripped me nude. Thankfully, Jackie got there first to gently lift my brief up and over my throbbing erection. But Angie quickly joined in the contest for my genitals and her hand, not Jackie's, managed to grip my penis.

Angie expertly stroked up and down. Just the right amount of pressure, just the right speed. "Ready to come?" she purred, her voice tickling the back of my neck. But Angie was looking to the side. The show was for Underhill. "Ready to come?" she repeated.

She wanted to show him what she could do.

"Mouths only," decreed Underhill.

Jackie started to kiss my nipple. Angie angled me sideways to Underhill, then plunged her mouth down my penis. Her oral skills were even more expert. I gritted my teeth, holding on. But my grip was weakening! I looked over at Underhill—

"Ring around the Rosie," he demanded.

Angie lifted her head and shot a frustrated look in Underhill's direction. Both women kissed around my body. Jackie kissed my balls and up and down my pole. It was so *soothing*. Then she slowly slid her lips down, sending me floating into whiteness. The clouds were soft and I went up and up and up.

Then far away, on another cloud, someone was singing. No, not someone, a whole choir. But not a church hymn. I heard Jackie's name.

I fluttered down from the clouds and opened my eyes. Jackie's bikini top was entirely off. Angie pulled at the strings holding her bikini bottom in place. One final tug dropped it to the mattress.

Exquisite loveliness shone forth from Jackie. Long black hair framed sparkling brown eyes and a gorgeous smile. Her beautiful breasts rose and fell with every breath, taut pointy nipples advertising the splendours of her soul. The orange, red, green and blue of the salamander atop her torso squeezed and released in carnal abandon.

Then Angie stepped forward and I had to move to one side to preserve eye contact.

"Spread your legs," Angie told her.

Jackie's eyes went wide in amazement. I moved to her side. Angie had at least two fingers inserted into Jackie's vagina. Jackie bit her lip and looked down. It was clear she wasn't enjoying herself, equally clear she wouldn't complain.

I put my hand on Angie's wrist. "Gentle, girl."

Angie wrenched her arm free—both from my hand and out of Jackie. Jackie gasped. She pressed her legs together.

Angie moved to one side and swatted Jackie on her bum.

"Ow!" protested Jackie.

"If you think lover boy can do better," smirked Angie, "spread your legs for him."

When Jackie remained motionless, Angie gave her another

swat. It was harder than the last, but Jackie didn't react. Instead her eyes, looked into mine. Emotion after emotion flashed across them, too quickly for me to identify them.

Angie readied another swat, but Jackie stepped to one side and shot her a menacing look. "Don't."

Angie lowered her arm.

Then Jackie turned to me and spread her legs. This time I could identify the emotion in her eyes. It was delight.

I stepped towards her. Even before I touched my hand between her thighs, I could tell that her genitals were warm and welcoming. When I touched the centre of her outer lips, a moan, almost inaudible, escaped her lips. She smiled. I pressed my finger forward. Jackie moaned again. Her whole body shuddered as my fingertip slipped inside.

Chapter 11 *Jackie*

My body quivered as Kyle touched my pussy. I tried to hold myself steady. *Everyone* was watching. His finger was electric. I caught ahold of some of the sensation, but I couldn't help but shudder as he slid in. One inch, two. Three, then the base of his hand touched the underside of my clit and his palm warmed as it gently caressed my pubic mound.

"Yes," I breathed, unable to help myself.

"Little slut," taunted Angie. "One touch and you're ready to come!" But her eyes were over my shoulder; the taunt was meant for Underhill, not me.

One touch—she was right, but only if done properly. Her own touch hadn't been right. Kyle's was. A groan escaped from deep within me. Bernie's had been; but Kyle's touch was somehow more profound. More about connection than technique.

Kyle's finger withdrew, invoking yearning even as it drew my insides together and stroked my pussy lips. Then its tip used my pussy juices to circle my clit, spinning desire and delight through her, through her and deep inside.

"Jackie, Jackie, cunt full of Kyle," taunted Angie in the same sing-song as Ring around the Rosie. She pinched my nipples. "Jackie, Jackie, tiny little titties."

Kyle's finger slipped down and entered me again. It was slippery, so I didn't feel much; nevertheless it drew us together. His touch seemed to mean something or was that just an idle hope? Once again, the base of his finger touched my clit and his palm pressed us together. But then he was pulling back.

"More," I pleaded.

This time, Kyle inserted two fingers. It wasn't the 'more' I'd been seeking, but still, it was wonderful. My clit ended up between his fingers and I gasped as he slid down her. I stumbled when he started to rotate his palm— He pulled himself out to use both hands to steady me.

'More' started to form on my lips—

"Ring around the Rosie, Pocket full of posies, Angie, Jackie, Kyle? This time it's *Kyle*!" Nara had led the song this time, mostly singing on her own, with only Bernie joining in at the last minute. I cursed at not being able to see them, to analyze the unfolding dynamics. I cursed at the cruel deprivation of my enjoyment of

Kyle's finger.

Angie roughly pulled Kyle between us. "Time for the fucking round," she told him. To me, she said, "You can pleasure him from behind." Angie flopped to the mattress, kneeling down, her bum high in the air, her pussy splayed wide in lewd invitation.

Kyle was about to drop down to his knees, but I quickly spun him away from Angie's licentious display. As soon as he had his back to her, I pulled him down to the mattress and guided his cock towards my bottom. "Please," I pleaded, then looked forward, adjusting myself to facilitate what I wanted Kyle to do.

His cock pressed against my pussy. I was just at the right state of arousal, wet, but not too wet. I felt his every inch as he slid into me. So gently. So gradually. So inexorably! All I could see was the mattress. Kyle inside me was heavenly; but still, being able to see Angie's face, at that moment, would have been even more heavenly!

Kyle stroked his cock in and out and I rocked my hips to accelerate his pleasure, to intensify my own. I started to float, but that wasn't what I wanted; I wanted to quicken his climb to his climax. I wanted to *possess* him!

Behind me, he shuddered and I smiled. But then I felt fingers slither around his balls and caress the shaft of my clit. Even with Kyle deep inside my pussy, Angie was interfering! I struggled to shake her off, but she was relentless. Every stroke on my clit made Kyle shudder. Angie reached her other hand around to caress the breast closest to her. Stroke after stroke and my connection with Kyle began to fade.

But other connections began to take hold of me. Hotter everywhere his cock touched as it slid in and out, hotter where her fingers fondled my breast, hotter where her fingers caressed my clit! Stroke after stroke and I was flesh, nothing but smoldering flesh. Hotter and hotter!

Power thundering from his cock. Electricity sparking from her fingers. My whole being was in the thrall of carnal sex. All that mattered was my clit and my cunt. Kyle's cock thrust me towards the edge. Angie's fingers spun me tighter and tighter.

I struggled to find Kyle but all I could see, all I could feel was the vortex being wrapped ever more tightly around me. Squeezing! Then squeezing right through me and I burst out, wave after wave thrashing me about. His hands anchored me close; her fingers whipped me back and forth so violently I shot into the sky. My body whipped back and forth so hard it almost shattered me into a million pieces.

His cock slammed in, and I was suddenly immobilized. My thighs and calves cramped into a solid mass. He wrenched himself out, crashing me back to earth. Her fingers sent wave after wave of orgasm up my spine. His thighs slapping against me gradually thawed my frozen legs, sending warm tremors down them and into my toes.

As wave after wave of pleasure coursed through me, the shudders that had possessed my body began to fade. His hands left my hips. Something warm trickled down my thighs. There was clapping. One pair of hands, then general applause. I suddenly remembered where I was and pulled myself forward. Kyle flopped out of me.

I collapsed, my back onto the mattress. Kyle was in embarrassed rapture. Angie was aroused and frustrated. I smiled at Kyle. He smiled back. But I had no idea what he was feeling. More to the point, what was *I* feeling?!?

Underhill and Joel went back to their computer. They gave themselves a 'high five' and motioned Nara over. Everyone else took that as their cue to leave. A quick gathering of clothes and Kyle and I followed the others out.

"Dock," whispered Kyle.

I nodded and flashed ten fingers.

He flashed ten fingers back and pointed at his watch.

Ten minutes later, Kyle emerged from behind a palm tree as I approached the dock. Hedonism's exhortation to be wicked for a week was dim in the early morning light. He was still wearing the same shirt and shorts as before. A soft quiver went up my spine as I remembered what was underneath his modest outfit. Momentarily, I wished I hadn't changed into jeans and a jacket. If I was still wearing my bikini—

"Something definitely went down tonight," he said, his voice barely above a whisper.

I nodded, unsure whether he meant our mutual orgasm or Underhill's latest machination.

"We should stake out Underhill's car," he continued. Crabs scurried across the dock.

I nodded, his meaning now clear. "I'll stake out their car."

"Okay, I'll stake out Underhill's room."

As I watched him walk away, part of me wished he'd been more fixated on what had happened between us that night, not what had happened behind the screen of Underhill's computer.

Thankfully, there was a deep shadow next to a building with a direct sight-line to Underhill's rental car. I scrunched myself as small as I could and waited. But dawn's early light was beginning to illuminate my hiding spot. If nothing happened in the next hour, I'd have to find a new hiding spot to keep watch on the black Camry.

My phone vibrated, the special vibration indicating an urgent call. I swiped right for my boss. "I need you here, *now!*" thundered his voice. So much for 'hello, how are you'.

"It's going down, now," I told him.

"You'll be going down, if you don't—"

"Ber—Underhill's on the run. We're going to arrest him this morning."

Silence. "You're sure?"

"Yes, I'm sure." Of course I *wasn't* sure!

Silence. "Okay." He rattled off a list of operational requirements, only a fraction of which registered.

Half an hour later, Joel emerged from the shadows carrying the laptop. If I could only rush up and tackle— Then Underhill and Nara came towards the car from the other direction. Joel handed the laptop to Nara, then got in to drive.

Kyle came up just as the car pulled out of the driveway. We looked back and forth between us. "Aren't you glad I rented a car?" I asked him.

At my car, we both headed for the driver's side. I dangled the keys.

"Have you ever driven on the left side of the road?" he asked.

I gave him the keys.

He drove quickly. As soon as we were a hundred yards down the road, he switched off the lights. It was dim, but Kyle was right to turn off the lights since Underhill would probably think it odd for another car to be out on the road behind him so early in the morning. A car approached and I wanted to go to the right to avoid a head-on collision. But Kyle was keeping to the left! I reached for the steering wheel, but the other car sailed safely past. On its proper side of the road.

He'd seen me reach for the wheel. "Slow down," I told him.

The smirk on his face needed wiping off. He did slow down, but just a touch.

Every few curves, we caught sight of Underhill's black Toyota.

But when we came to a small town, he didn't slow down at all. "Slow down," I told him.

"Underhill didn't."

"You'll hit someone." There were pedestrians walking along the side of the road. Occasionally someone darted across.

"We don't want to lose him."

"There's only one road. You can speed up once we get out of town."

He did slow down. Except when someone wanted to turn into our lane. "It's not a contest!" I told him.

"That's where you're wrong. In Jamaica, driving is a contest of manhood."

Finally we escaped out of town. The sky was getting lighter. There were two cars ahead of us. But Underhill was nowhere to be seen. "Speed up," I told him.

Kyle grunted and the car shot forward.

After ten minutes of tense driving, we managed to pass the two cars in front of us. I was glad Kyle was driving; my instincts as to which side to pass on were totally wrong. But he was still driving too fast.

"Slow down," I told him.

"Underhill's going to escape."

"How do you know?"

"It's what he's always done."

"There's only one airport."

"There are *three* airports on the north coast. If we don't catch up with him, he could shoot past Montego Bay and head for one of the other two."

"You were with him when I arrived."

He shot me a look then jerked his head back to the road. "What's that supposed to mean?"

"I still haven't been able to confirm your story with Washington."

"I haven't been able to confirm your story either."

"We should call in now."

Kyle shook his head. "If we call in before they arrive at

airport, Morant will just invent an emergency, just like he did when he had you arrested."

"I have an agent seconded to the Constabulary Force at the airport."

"He's still under Morant's control. We have to wait until the R.C.M.P. liaison arrives."

I looked over at him. Was he worried that the F.B.I. would take all the credit, or was he just being careful?

I caught sight of the outskirts of Montego Bay in the distance. "But if we're too late—"

"Underhill can't be too much further ahead. We have to wait until the warrant for his arrest arrives."

I nodded. Kyle had a point. The R.C.M.P. liaison officer was bringing the warrant on the first incoming flight of the day.

"There!" I pointed. There was a black sedan. Way in the distance. It certainly looked like Underhill's Toyota Camry.

After a few minutes of break-neck driving we pulled closer. My knuckles almost popped from crushing the door handle. Kyle squinted at the license plate. "It's them!" he proclaimed.

A large jet thundered overhead, preparing to land. "And there's our warrant!" We turned and smiled at each other.

I speed-dialed my agent at the airport and put him on speaker. "Prepare to arrest Underhill," I told him.

My phone squawked. "I can't. We're on standby waiting for a small plane to land. Morant says they have solid intel that it's full of cocaine."

"I need you at the main entrance!" I swore under my breath, hoping that Kyle hadn't heard my voice crack.

Kyle slammed his hand on the steering wheel. "We have no choice but to involve the Jamaican Constabulary Force's Corruption Unit."

We both knew that the Corruption Unit had been infiltrated by everyone it was supposed to be investigating. It was rumored that half it officers were working for the other side.

I nodded and readied to dial. But Kyle shook his head. "Call my guy on the plane. He should be on the tarmac by now. He may know who's clean and who's not."

Underhill's Camry pulled up to the departure entrance. He, Joel and Nara jumped out. No luggage. Just Joel carrying the laptop. Parking enforcement officers started to swarm the black

Toyota. We pulled up just behind and dashed in after Underhill. A parking enforcement officer grabbed Kyle's arm, but he shook him off, pointed at our rental car and dashed inside the building.

My F.B.I. credentials slowed the rest of the parking enforcement crew just long enough for me to follow Kyle inside.

Underhill, Joel and Nara were in line to check in for their flight. They didn't seem to have noticed us. Kyle waved me to one side. "Call my guy," he said.

I called. There was a jumble of cross-talk as we each tried to describe where we were. Finally Kyle's man understood. Underhill worked himself to the front of the line. Joel slapped down three sets of documents. Kyle's man waved at us from the far end of the concourse. We waved him towards us.

I called the Jamaican Corruption Unit. This was going to go down fast. If Underhill had a man inside the corruption unit, he wouldn't have time to react. Then all three of us made a mad dash to the counter where Underhill was checking in. Kyle and I arrived first, just as Underhill was turning around, his check-in complete. I held up my F.B.I. credentials. "F.B.I.!" I shouted. "You're under arrest."

"This is Jamaica, dearie," smirked Underhill. "Not Miami." He looked back and forth between Kyle and I. "Go back home to your corrupt hypocrites." His voice was sharp with sarcasm.

Kyle's man slid to a stop to our left. "George Steele, Royal Canadian Mounted Police. I have an Interpol arrest warrant for Bernard Underhill, Joel Ritchie, Nara Takahashi and Shaneese Campbell." He held up a single sheet of paper. Steele was tall and thin, his hair cropped short. His speech was as precise as it was polite.

Underhill grabbed at the paper, but Steele pulled it behind him. Suddenly the warrant vanished from Steele's hand. We turned to follow it and ended up staring into the fierce eyes of Inspector Morant. "I am the only one authorized to make an arrest here."

"But—Interpol—Warrant," Kyle, George and I sputtered.

Underhill ran away to our right, towards the departure lounge. Joel and Nara followed. We tried to give chase, but a phalanx of Morant's uniformed officers barred the way.

"Interpol! Warrant! He's getting away!" we sputtered.

"*Interpol*," mimicked Morant. Then he waved to his lieutenant. "Arrest them for impersonating police officers."

Three undercover officers burst through the door down the hall—yes, cops can tell cops—but Underhill sidestepped them. However, one of the officers, on the theory that anyone running must be a bad guy, tackled Underhill. Joel tried to pull the officer off. A rather entertaining melee ensued.

"Arrest them!" bellowed Morant, waving in the direction of the melee. "Assault and provoking a riot."

Morant's lieutenant, and his officers, sped down the hall. Since we were no longer restrained, we followed. Morant followed, wheezing, "Stop! Stop!"

Just as Morant's lieutenant reached the melee, one of the undercover officers held up his badge. "Jamaica Constabulary Force, Corruption Unit. Arrest these men."

Morant's lieutenant knew better than to tussle with the corruption unit. Underhill was handcuffed. But Joel broke free and activated the laptop. Two officers grabbed him.

Kyle and I grabbed the laptop. Numbers and letters were flashing across the screen in every direction.

"It's a decryption algorithm," said Joel. "Every file is being deconstructed into bits and bytes. Absolutely, absolutely unreadable."

Kyle twisted Joel's left arm behind his back. "Stop it," he demanded.

"Can't be done," Joel sneered.

I tried, but the numbers and letters kept coming. The laptop was getting hot. I tried every combination of keys I could think of. Numbers and letters overwhelmed the screen, turning it into one bright white light. Hot! Burning! My hand! I dropped the laptop. It clattered to the floor. Part of it was on fire. Everyone looked at it, stunned.

"You don't have any evidence," asserted Underhill. "We demand that you let us go."

Steele grabbed his warrant back from Morant. "We have an Arrest Warrant from Interpol."

The leader of the corruption unit squad told Underhill that he was under arrest. "The details will be worked out in due course."

Morant shrugged, gathered his men, and left.

Another tourist arrived and spoke to Steele, then came over to us.

"Antoine," said Kyle.

Antoine pointed to my tan line. "*Joli bronzage*, Martini" said Antoine. He angled his head towards me. "Who is *la belle femme*?" Then he turned to me, smiled, and extended his hand. "Antoine Jonquiére *à votre service*."

"Jennifer Logan, F.B.I.," I said. Antoine turned back to Kyle who was apparently the lesser of two evils.

"Are you going to stay?" asked Kyle.

"I just escort da *prisonnier*." He returned to Underhill.

"Antoine's a fellow Mountie," said Kyle.

Steele came over and shook Kyle's hand, something Antoine hadn't done. Both of the newly-arrived Mounties went with the corruption squad, their big fish in the middle. Underhill, Ritchie and Takahashi were led off in single file, their wrists handcuffed together. The press came and snapped photos. Underhill was finally being forced to undergo a perp walk!

Kyle and I stared down, morosely, at Underhill's still smoldering laptop.

My phone beeped.

It was a text from the decryption squad. They'd unscrambled what I'd downloaded on my flash drive and were sifting through reams and reams of documents. I turned my phone to Kyle. His eyes shot wide as the message penetrated. We hugged and walked away from the burning remains of Joel's laptop. A squad of firemen ran past us towards the flames.

On the ride back to the Negril, Kyle—Keith—and I chattered a mile a minute until all the adrenaline washed out of our bodies. Then we lapsed into a reflective silence. I was slowly shedding Jackie Warne and returning to Jennifer Logan. Jackie was a free-spirited sex-pot. Jennifer was a strait-laced F.B.I. Agent who chose her acquaintances so well she didn't have any outside law enforcement. And hooking up with a fellow federal agent was far too dangerous career-wise.

I loved my job—putting Underhill behind bars had been stupendous!—but my personal life sucked. I was shriveling up inside. I glanced over at Keith. Changing emotions flickered across his face. I wished I knew what he was thinking. He made me feel safe and secure. Kyle—Keith—had begun to unlock feelings I hadn't felt in years. Decades? He was several hours away by plane. But he was safely in the law enforcement category. And he wasn't a federal agent.

Keith negotiated a sharp turn and I had to grip the door handle. When I turned back to him, his jaw was set, as if he was mulling a set of unattractive alternatives. I wondered if any of them involved me?

As we entered the lobby back at Hedo, the receptionist waved me over. "A package was delivered for you," he told me.

I ripped it open. It was a set of airline tickets to Washington D.C. for Johnny, Shaneese, Angie, Lydia, and Nara. I handed Nara's over to Keith. "This one you can rip up."

As Keith tore the ticket into as many little pieces as he could, I scanned the covering letter. I was to attempt to persuade the rest of Underhill's crew to co-operate with our investigation. The Justice Department was reviewing a possible plea bargain. In the meantime, I was to hold onto the airline tickets.

In the dining room, Kyle waved a waiter over and whispered something into his ear. I marched to Underhill's table where only Johnny was in attendance. Johnny looked me up and down, but Kyle stepped in front of me and turned Johnny's chin and roving eyes to him: "Bernie said to gather everyone here for dinner. There's going to be an important announcement. Free time until dinner."

Johnny looked back and forth between us. Kyle raised an eyebrow. Johnny scooted off. The waiter Kyle had spoken to brought a bottle of Underhill's special Champagne over to the table and made a show of popping the cork.

Kyle handed me a glass of bubbly and began to pour his. I gently gripped the bottle and set it on the table. "I want to celebrate," I told him. Most of the adrenaline from the excitement of Underhill's capture had left my bloodstream, but its residual effects were still bouncing around inside me. There was only one way to get rid of it. Please, please, let Kyle feel the same way.

"I want to celebrate too." His glass had only an inch of golden sparkles in it, but he reached for it. I covered the top of his glass with my key card.

He raised an eyebrow. But behind it there was uncertainty, not the harsh look he'd given Johnny. He was intrigued. And there was something more, but I couldn't put my finger on it. My invitation couldn't have been more obvious. Half of me wanted to kick myself, the other half was consumed by desire and didn't care.

Kyle—Keith?—took my key card, put it into his pocket, and pulled me to my feet. He wrapped his arm around me and we strolled towards my room. I wanted to skip, to dance, to run as quickly to the kingdom of carnal delights as possible. Instead, I listened to my heart pound inside my chest and relaxed against the muscular frame striding us slowly forward.

Keith popped my door open and for an instant I thought he was going to pick me up to carry me across the threshold. But we both stepped into the room on our own two feet.

As soon as the door clicked shut behind us, I pulled my shirt up and over my head. My fingers flew to the button on my jeans, but his hands stopped me.

"We have time," he murmured. He slowly undid the button and pulled the zipper down, making sure not to touch me.

I jumped backwards onto the bed and squirmed to the top, half removing my jeans. He took them the rest of the way off, folded them and put them on the dresser.

"We have time," he chuckled.

"And I don't want to waste a moment of it." I reached around behind me, unclasped my bra and threw it towards my jeans. Keith caught it in mid-air, folded it, and placed it atop my jeans.

I reached for my panties. He wagged a finger at my crotch. "Don't you dare."

I left my hand in place, but kept it motionless. He began to unbutton his shirt. "Faster," I told him.

He didn't speed up. Finally his shirt was folded neatly on the dresser next to my jeans and bra. He undid the button on his pants.

I started to pull my panties down. He shook his head and kept his hands motionless. I removed my hands, holding them palm up towards him. He undid the button and pulled the zipper downwards.

This was torture. I wanted him. I wanted Keith like I'd never *wanted* a man before. My whole body was hot. My nipples screamed every time I took a breath they were so hard. Every inch of me cried out for his touch. My pussy was a boiling mass of *desire*. Surely he could see how wet I was!

It was impossible to remove a pair of pants any slower than Keith removed his. As soon as they were folded atop his shirt, I yanked my panties off my feet. They sailed past his hand, hit the mirror and dropped down to the dresser. He raised an eyebrow and picked them up. The bastard knows how wet I am! It took all my willpower not to pound my fists on the mattress as Keith carefully folded my panties and placed them atop my bra.

His briefs were light blue. Ordinary cotton. But on him they looked splendid. Even more splendid was the erection pressing forward inside them, and even more splendid than that was the fact that the force his erection was exerting on his waist band, pulling it away from his body. He wanted me as much as I wanted him!

"You look magnificent," I told him.

"Not as magnificent as you." His eyes caressed my body, making my belly tighten.

I opened my legs. "Let me see all of you." I feasted on his broad shoulders, on his tight chest, on the muscles in his arms readying to crush and caress me.

He teased a finger under the top of his brief. "Is that all you want, to look?"

"I showed you mine."

He removed his briefs, turning sideways in the process. I quivered at the sight of Keith's slim waist, round bum. His protruding cock sent little sparks up my spine.

Then he turned facing me, his cock throbbing. "Is that all you want, to look?" he repeated. Hunger clenched at me, hunger to have his cock throb inside me.

"Focus on your own desires," I told him rocking my hips up and down. "Your cock is throbbing with desire. You want to plunge it inside me. You *need* to plunge it inside me."

"Maybe I just like the way you look at me, your eyes dreamy with desire." His face was hard, like a wolf anticipating fresh meat.

"Wait until you see what my eyes look like when they're watching your butt clench as you plunge your cock into my pussy!" I pointed to the mirror above the bed.

Finally Keith got the message. Every muscle in his body contracted, just a bit, but unmistakably. His eyes narrowed into little slits. The hunter's focus. His eyes raked up my body. A twinge in my pussy. No air in my lungs. Then his eyes locked into mine, pinning me hard against the mattress.

He climbed atop the bed. His hands on either side of my right leg, then straddling my torso. His knees moved up between my legs. I wanted to move, to welcome his advance. But his eyes paralyzed me. I breathed, but only because he willed me to breathe. Then his lips were on mine and he sucked all the air out of my lungs. I gave up my life force to him, willingly. My heart stopped. Then he made me breathe again.

His weight was atop me, not heavy, just there. Warm. Fulfilling. His cock nuzzled up and down my pussy lips. Not invading, just greeting.

"Please," I begged.

"Please?"

"Please, Kyle! Keith! Please fuck me!"

"Hard?"

"Hard!"

"Fast?"

"As hard and as fast as you possibly can!"

His cock plunged. So swiftly I was unaware until he mashed his pubic bone into mine. I was momentarily aware of the searing heat of him filling me. Then he was out. Thrusting in. Jerking out. He plunged and lurched, throwing me this way and that on the mattress.

Finally I managed to push myself upwards just as he was dropping himself back into me. He was a raging bull atop me, but now I was able to meet his mad passion with my own. My entire sex was on fire and I wanted to spread the flames to him, to consume him as he was consuming me.

Then he grabbed me and held me tight. One hand on my butt, the other around my shoulders. He kissed me. I couldn't breathe. I couldn't move. All I could do was watch his butt muscles pumping himself into me. Hard and fast and furiously they pumped, clenching and releasing, screwing themselves into a little ball pressing forward hard into me. Then releasing outward. Then tightening taut pressing into me.

I was in the mirror, I was in his butt, I was in his cock. I was cock and pussy. I was storming lust. Lightning and hurricane and heat.

His butt clenched even harder, screwing around to the right. His butt was a tornado, drilling deeper and deeper into me. And I was tighter and tighter around his cock each time it plunged into me.

Chapter 12 *Keith*

"Focus on your own desires," she said. Not that she was giving me much of a choice, the way she was rocking her hips up and down.

"Maybe I just like the way you look at me, your eyes dreamy with desire," I told her, trying to keep my expression neutral.

"Wait until you see what my eyes look like when they're watching your butt clench as you plunge your cock into my pussy!" She pointed to the mirror above the bed.

My eyes devoured her. The way her eyes were pulling blood into my genitals, I couldn't help it. A wide smile illuminated her face. Long black hair floated over her right shoulder. The tail of her tattoo wrapped around her breast then sucked me along its body into her glowing vulva. Her thighs tightened, readying. Blood surged into every muscle in my body, flooding then with the energy they were about to expend.

I knelt on the bed and crawled upward, her eyes urging me forward. I was powerless to resist. She drew my lips to hers and we kissed. Her body drew me to hers and our skin touched—chest, tummy, hips, thighs. My penis brushed against the warm moist entrance to heaven.

"Please," she begged. *She wanted me as much as I wanted her!?!*

"Please?"

"Please, Kyle! Keith! Please fuck me!" *Yikes!*

"How do you--?"

"Hard!"

"Fast?"

"As hard and as fast as you possibly can!"

I pushed myself inside, intending to be gentle despite her exhortation, but I slipped all the way in and before I could pull back I was mashing our pubic bones together. She was warm and wet and tight! Hot lust washed over me. I plunged in and out and in, jerking thrusts over and over. I was lust. She was lust. She rocked her hips, accelerating my thrusts. We thrashed about the mattress, lust lurching us this way and that.

I almost slipped out of her, so I grabbed upwards on her bum and cradled her shoulders. We kissed. I couldn't breathe. Only my glutes were moving, pumping into her. I stroked in and out of her, in and out of her tight little hot pot.

The more I pumped, the harder I pumped, the faster I pumped, the wilder she became beneath me. I tried to hold her tight, but each time I plunged myself inside her, the more she sweated, the looser my grip became.

I paused for a moment, trying to readjust my position. It was just for an instant, but it was all Jackie needed, all Jennifer needed. She slithered out from underneath me, then used my efforts to hold myself inside her and to hold her close, to turn me onto my back.

"Jackie."

"Jennifer."

"Jennifer."

"Keith."

"Jenny."

On top of me, she was a maelstrom, spreading her legs and plummeting down my pole, then sucking rapidly up, then down again. In one swift motion, she clenched her legs together and between mine. Hands on my arms stopped me from hugging her. Her whole body stiffened in a descending wave, from the tribal tattoo between her shoulder blades, down her spine, between the globes of her magnificent bum and ending up in her powerful thighs. Over and over she undulated, using my pole as her fulcrum. Over and over she milked up and down its length.

Just when I'd finally got my breath, Jennifer pulled her hands sideways down my arms and pressed her whole body into mine. Her piercings burned into my chest. Her lips sucked air out of my lungs followed by her tongue playing with my efforts to breathe. I could only lie back and watch the length of her body in the mirror above us, the length of her body caressing and squeezing and rocking and swaying.

Her breaths came in little gasps with each stroke of her vagina. I managed to gasp in time with her. She was getting warmer and warmer. Sweat trickled down her spine. Her bum clenched and released in a frenzy, as if possessed. It clenched and squeezed, possessing me.

Finally I got my arms free. My hands wanted to grab her luscious bum. But my eyes forbade any obstruction. My eyes wanted to feast on the single-minded fury of what her glute muscles were doing to me, on the pleasure she was extracting from me.

Jenny lifted herself up and her eyes bore into mine. "Are you ready to come?"

I shook my head. I wanted this to last forever and forever. She slowed and we breathed together. Deep breaths, cooling, nourishing. She had transitioned us from sweaty sex to making love. I wanted to hug her forever, but my arms were lead on the bed.

"Jenny," I said, possessing her soul by speaking her name.

"Keith," she said, weaving us together, intertwining our beings.

Sparkles danced in her eyes. Her smile made me gasp. "Look at my breasts." They were swollen, her nipples pressing against the golden knobs of her barbells. Below she twisted and accelerated her strokes.

"No!" I cried.

"Yes!"

"No!" Please don't end this, please!

"Yes!" She twisted again, keeping up her pace. Her face scrunched with every stroke. She had found the spot.

"No!"

"Yes!" Her face told me she would not be denied.

"No!" But little spasms at the base of my penis—

"Yes!"

"Yes!" I shot myself into her.

"Yes!" Her whole body tensed, rigid.

I whipped her beneath me and plunged myself into her, aiming for the spot she'd found. The exertion reduced me to animal grunts.

"Yes!" she screamed, thrashing on the bed. But I held her tight, thrusting in and out as fast as I could. Her whole body was one large spasm. My hands slid off her sweat. But her spasm let me regain control. I pumped my pole into her. I pumped my life force into her. And she swallowed it up.

After an eternity, she calmed and our bodies undulated along each other, like waves in the ocean making love. One breath from our mouths to our toes. Mother ocean making love for all eternity.

She looked dreamily up into my eyes. "Kyle," she breathed.

I rolled her onto her side and held her close. "Keith."

"Keith," she repeated.

"Jennifer."

"It sounds nice when you say my name."

We lay together in the afterglow, not talking, hardly

breathing. Even the slightest movement might bring us back to reality, to the here and now of our lives. I wanted to stay in this hidden time, in her room, in her bed, in her arms forever. Every time a thought of going back home intruded into my consciousness, of what might happen to my career, I pushed it away.

I knew I should ask her about herself. I knew Jackie. I barely knew anything about Jennifer. But all I wanted to do was to hug her close, to feel her heart beating against my skin, to hear the murmur of air entering and escaping her lungs.

Outside, feet clattered up the stairs. But they were outside, where they couldn't hear us. Knuckles rapped on Jennifer's door. She stirred. "Shhh," I told her. "They'll go away."

The knuckles rapped again. Three times insistent. She sat up, almost out of my arms. I pulled her back down. The knuckles rapped again. "Agent Logan?" whispered a voice.

This time Jennifer bolted upright and whirled onto the floor. She pulled her jeans, Tee and jacket on, like a tornado spinning them onto her body. She motioned frantically for me to gather my clothes and get into the bathroom. She spun around to ensure that all evidence of our coupling had been hidden, then walked to the door. I shut the bathroom door, except for a crack. I quickly pulled my clothes on, in case Jennifer might need my help.

A man in a suit and tie came into the room. "Agent Logan?" he asked.

"Special Agent Jennifer Logan. And you are?"

He flashed identification. "Larry Chipman, Justice." He handed over a letter-sized envelope which Jennifer opened. "As you can see, the Justice Department has agreed that no charges will be brought against the rest of Bernard Underhill's associates so long as they co-operate with your investigation and agree to testify against him."

Chipman was still there when dinnertime rolled around. Jennifer was dressed as formally as he was and I suddenly felt out-of-place in my tee shirt and shorts. Jennifer was in full special-agent mode. Jackie had been in-your-face fun and games. Jennifer was more professional, formal.

Jennifer gathered Angie, Lydia, Johnny and Shaneese together over dinner. I sat at the end of the table and let Special Agent Logan do her thing. Chipman sat off to one side, not participating, not eating, but watching carefully. He'd delivered the letter of authority Jennifer had needed. Why hadn't he returned to Washington?

Jackie showed the airline tickets to the four remaining members of Underhill's crew. "You can use these and be picked up on your arrival to Washington D.C.. If you testify against Underhill, there will be no charges brought against you. *Or* you can stay here and take your chances with the Jamaican police."

Underhill's stragglers hesitated. Johnny looked back and forth between the women. They ignored him. He sighed and took the ticket being proffered by Jennifer. Angie and Shaneese shot him a dirty look. Lydia took a ticket. Angie flung dirty looks at her, then at me. Shaneese glowered at Jennifer.

"Jamaican jails are not Club Fed," said Jennifer. Angie and Shaneese haughtily took the remaining tickets.

After dinner I took Jennifer aside, but she was standoffish. She angled her head towards Chipman who was staring at us. Creepy. "He can't see us touching," she told me.

"What?!"

"Underhill spilled the beans about my having sex with him. And with you. My conduct is being evaluated."

"But you brought down—"

"And now I may be brought down."

"I have to go to Ottawa tomorrow. I thought…"

Jennifer reached her hand out to touch my arm, but quickly withdrew it, fighting not to turn towards Chipman. She looked scared, torn. And for the first time since I'd met her, tentative. "Ottawa?"

"For my disciplinary hearing."

"But you brought Underhill down. Surely—"

I shook my head. "My bosses are even more sticklish than yours. Their superiors won't have time to absorb and analyze Underhill's arrest before my hearing."

She looked sad. "Keith. I'm sorry."

I gave Chipman a sharp look. The look I reserved for lawyers. Then I turned back to Jennifer. "Surely he can't object to us talking?"

She shook her head.

I angled my eyes sideways. Chipman was still watching us. I suddenly wished that Antoine had come to Hedo instead of accompanying Steele and the prisoner back north. Jennifer was fidgeting. "What's going to happen after you leave here?" I asked.

"There'll be the standard F.B.I. debriefing. I'll be reprimanded for having sex while undercover. They may place me on restricted duty. If Justice complains that I've compromised their case, I may face further disciplinary action."

"Justice wouldn't have had a case without you."

"They tend not to see things that way. What's going to happen to you?"

"I've stepped on a lot of toes over the years, cut a lot of corners. If I'm lucky I'll keep my pension."

There was a moment of silence as we each contrasted the bleak desert of our lives with the hibiscus blooms glowing red beneath palm trees swaying in Jamaica's tropical breeze.

"I liked working with you," I told her.

"I liked—I like being with you."

"When we had sex—"

"I liked that too." There was a momentary sparkle in her eyes. But then sadness. And her sadness emphasized the past tense she'd used.

"When we were together, in your room, was that the excitement of the moment, or...?" I felt like an awkward teenager, but I had to know.

"It was both, Keith." She touched my arm and let her fingers linger. We smiled at each other. The hell with Chipman.

"Do you have a boyfr—a significant other back in D.C.?"

She shook her head. "No, there's no one. You?"

"I divorced five years ago. I have a daughter. Since the divorce..."

"Sex, but no one who mattered."

I nodded.

"Same with me." She withdrew her hand.

"What if you mattered to me?" I wanted to kick myself for taking awkward to a *whole* new level.

Chapter 13 *Jennifer*

"What if you mattered to me?" asked Keith. He watched me, waiting for an answer.

"What if you mattered to *me*?" I knew it wasn't proper to answer a question with a question, but I needed time to think.

"I'd like that."

"I'd like that too." To hell with waiting, with thinking. For once, I should just listen to my heart. I touched him briefly, then withdrew my hand. Chipman was watching, and *he* mattered too, especially if my career mattered.

Keith watched my hand retreat. "But?"

"But it's complicated." I angled my head towards Chipman.

"Is he your—"

"Boyfriend? No! I just met him now."

"Then?"

"He'll file a report. Back home, I never touch men. I never flirt. Never. Not even a hint. Back home, they're going to read what Underhill says I did. Chipman's observations will put that in context."

"Which Jennifer do you like? Jamaica Jennifer or Washington Jennifer?"

"That's the problem. I like both."

That quieted him for a moment and finally I had time to think. 'I like both' wasn't the whole story. There were things I didn't like about either. I didn't like the process of opening my legs to any and every cock that just popped up. Sex should have love mixed in with it. But I didn't like the all work and no play pigeon-hole I'd been boxed into at the F.B.I.. My legs were suddenly weak. I found two chairs and we sat down.

"We made love three times..." His tone was pensive.

I did my best to match his tone, to remove as much rebuke as I could. "We had *sex* three times."

"But didn't you—"

"Not the first two times, no."

"But you must have felt *something*?"

"I felt a big strong man who wanted to please me, to *pleasure* me as a woman. I felt a big strong man who wanted to make me feel safe. And you did make me feel safe. And it was intensely pleasurable and sexy and arousing and orgasmic. But it was part of a situation. It was physical."

"No emotion? Absolutely none?"

"I felt cared for. I felt immense tenderness. Deep affection. But romantic love? No."

"But you can't divorce the act from the emotion." He winced at the word 'divorce'.

"When you jerk off, do you feel love?"

"Who says I jerk off?" There was a wry smile at the edge of his lips.

"Answer the question."

"No. But I'm alone. I'm not—"

"Was there emotion when you were with Angie?"

"Angie?"

"I saw how she looked at you when you were paying attention to me. Did you feel love when you were with Angie?"

He shook his head.

"Because you were just trying to pump her for information."

He nodded, hurt playing across his face.

I gave him a gentle poke to his ribs, angling my body so that Chipman couldn't see. "But you didn't ask me about the third time."

He didn't take the bait. "Underhill is reputed to be quite the ladies' man."

"The reputation is well deserved."

"I could never be like him."

"I should hope not!"

"I meant that I don't think I'll ever be as good a lover as Underhill."

"I don't think that Underhill ever made love in his life."

"Just sex?"

"Just sex."

"But fantastic, mind-blowing sex?"

I nodded. "If you like that sort of thing."

"Wouldn't any woman?"

I shrugged. "Probably, but after a while it's just an empty physical act."

"It doesn't matter who you're with, it's just sex?"

"Sometimes you have sex with someone because you like them."

"It doesn't have to be love?"

"No. What about the last time we... Do you like me?"

"Very much." Wistful.

"But you weren't in love?"

He shook his head and his whole body shuddered. He turned, starting to get up.

"Keith."

He stopped and turned to me, but he didn't sit back down.

"You didn't ask how I felt when I invited you back to my room. The third time, when we…"

"And if I was to ask you about that, the third time, what would you say?"

"When I asked you up, I knew that I liked you."

He sat back down. "And later?"

"I knew I liked you a lot."

"How much later?"

I batted my eyes seductively and we both laughed.

"Would you like to come up?" He asked. "To my room this time?"

My head jerked towards Chipman. He was watching us intently, taking notes. "If *he* wasn't here, in a heartbeat."

Keith's tradecraft was excellent. He didn't turn even a quarter inch towards Chipman. "If Chipman weren't here," he breathed, "would you kiss me?"

"If Chipman wasn't here, I'd kiss you so long and so deeply that you'd see stars."

"You'd have to throw me in the ocean to revive me."

"I'd blow air into your lungs and once you were breathing again, I'd dive beneath the waves to blow something else."

"You're a naughty girl."

"You bring the naughtiness out in me."

"I'd bring you up out of the water and hug you close."

"You'd have to be standing to hug me."

He nodded. "But the salt water would slide your lizard—"

"—Salamander—"

"—salamander down to the tip of my penis."

"She does like to swallow things."

"Even long and pokey things?

"Especially long and pokey things!"

"Down her throat I'd slide."

"Right in the ocean?"

"If Chipman weren't here."

"Would you have the endurance?"

"For you? Most certainly! I'd slide you up and down."

"Pulling and tugging—"

"On your tits and your tit piercings."

"And below—"

"Especially down below, rotating and mashing in warm mother ocean."

"Would you have the endurance?"

"I would have the endurance to make you scream my name to the heavens!"

"Keith."

"Louder."

"If Chipman wasn't here—"

"—I'd make you scream so loud the stars would shake."

"Keith."

"Jennifer." His whisper tickled down the back of my neck.

"My body would be salty."

"I'd lick every inch until you were cleaner than clean."

"If Chipman wasn't here."

"I'd carry you to my room."

"Such energy you have."

"You give me energy."

"And in your room, what would you do?"

"If Chipman weren't here?"

"Yes… If…"

"In my room, I'd throw you on my bed."

"What if I tried to run away?"

"I'd look deep into your eyes, express my feelings for you, draw out your feelings for me."

"You'd quiver?"

"Quiver?"

"You'd shake all over and open your body, open your soul to me."

"And we'd make love."

"What would it be like?"

"Shut your eyes."

I shut my eyes.

"Every breath you take, you'd feel me."

"Yes!" And I *did* feel him.

"I'd touch your tummy and draw your breath out through

your belly button."

"Keith, I—"

"And then I'd push it back in."

"There are other things you can push in."

"Jennifer. Are you thinking naughty thoughts again?"

"You bring them out."

"So you're imagining something being pushed in *and* pulled out?"

"Yes," I gasped. We were *just talking* and I *gasped*!

"Special Agent Logan?"

It wasn't Keith's—my eyes rocketed open.

Keith was standing to one side. Chipman was right in front of me. "Our car is here," he announced.

Ten minute later, ten excruciating minutes, I stood on my tiptoes and said goodbye to Keith with a kiss. I couldn't care less what Chipman might write in his report.

But once back on the ground in D.C., it became quite clear that everyone in Washington *did* care. I was put through the wringer: a week of debriefing and another week of meeting after meeting discussing my behavior. The only way I got through it was to Skype with Keith every night. Sometimes he pretended to be Kyle. We found some *creative* camera angles!

But at the end, I was given a choice: break off any relationship I might have developed with Keith Martin or resign my position with the Federal Bureau of Investigation. It seemed that Justice had decided that if it could be shown that everything down in Jamaica had been an act, Underhill wouldn't be able to taint my testimony. And in their mind, 'everything' included Kyle.

I was given two weeks of paid leave to think about it.

Chapter 14 *Keith*

Ottawa, in the dying days of winter, was bleak and cold. Everything was grey, from the sidewalks to the dirty snow lining them. As the nation's capital, the city was overrun by civil servants. Half of them were morose all the time, even on the odd day when the sun came out. The other half, the ones who put in a relaxed 9-5 and not a minute more, were tired but happy. They viewed work as a time to rest up from non-stop partying.

My disciplinary hearing had gone pretty much as expected. The lawyer appointed on my behalf by the Mounted Police Association had done her best. But she'd been overwhelmed by all the petty allegations of my past misconduct which had been dredged up. When she'd tried to deal with one, they'd blindsided her with another. It had been a game of whack-a-mole which had left both of us exhausted and disoriented.

My superior officers blunted the effect of my participation in the successful operation to bring Underhill down. In their eyes, had it not been for the intervention of the Americans, my unsanctioned operation would have blown up in our faces and damaged the R.C.M.P.'s working relationship with the Jamaican Constabulary Force. Worries about Jamaican gangs and telephone scam artists operating in Canada apparently trumped international child trafficking. Only a letter from Jennifer on very official looking F.B.I. letterhead extolling my virtues and professionalism had kept me from being fired altogether.

As it was, serial disobedience of orders meant that my superior managed to shake me loose and have me banished to a desk job in Ottawa. I was relegated to pushing paper to assist other officers in their investigations rather than conducting investigations of my own. The worst part of the job was its limited workload. It gave me far too much time for thinking and reflection.

Only Jennifer's nightly Skype calls had kept me going. But then she said that she needed time to sort things out and even those rays of sunshine vanished from my life.

So, I'd joined a gym and started training to run a marathon. I was running past the courthouse when I noticed an officer who I'd helped with an investigation. Her face had been plastered all over the papers.

She was being interviewed for the evening news. "What is

the accused being charged with?" asked the reporter.

"He defrauded homeowners and construction companies by mixing inferior products in with his cement and by then marketing it as premium grade."

"How did you break the case?"

"We acquired and analyzed the accused's purchasing records over a three year period and compared them with his sales records."

Those were the documents I'd sourced! And the analysis I'd performed. My heart skipped a beat. At least I'd done *something* worthwhile. I straightened my sweats as best I could, anticipating a few moments of camaraderie with another Mountie.

After the reporter left, I stepped forward. "Hi, I'm Keith—"

"Hi, Keith. Did you want me to start at the beginning, or did you have a specific question?" She favoured me with the same smile she'd used on the other reporter. She didn't even recognize me. I mumbled 'congratulations' and jogged off.

When I got to the bridge, I sprinted to the middle then stared down at the Ottawa river. Flowing inexorably to god knows where. Like my life. Flowing to who knows where. Flowing to who gives a damn.

That night, Jennifer called on Skype. "Hi, Keith," she began, then launched into our usual introductory chit chat. She was so beautiful! Her lips were soft. Like they were when she kissed me. Her camera cut out, but I could still see her face, her face with Jamaican palm trees waving in the breeze behind her.

She finished and I contributed the minutiae of my day. Then, as always we paused. The person with the most important item of news was to go next.

Jennifer cleared her throat. "They said I had to break up with you as a condition of my reinstatement."

My heart fell down to the pit of my stomach. "I've been reinstated as well," I told her. Then I described the cement fraud case in detail, omitting my limited involvement in the investigation.

She tried to get her camera working, but couldn't. She told me she was going away for a few days. And on that note, my crappiest of crappy days ended.

The next day I threw myself into my work. Only seven more years to go until retirement.

After work, I took a new route for my daily run. Half a kilometer in, there was a poster promising a free gift for attending a real estate speculation seminar. I memorized the number and briefly fantasized about becoming a property mogul.

Lightning flashed in the distance. The sky darkened, only to be illuminated by another flash of lightning. It began to rain. Each clap of thunder was getting closer. I thought about seeking shelter, then remembered the long odds of being hit by lightning and kept going. The odds of being hit were about the same as winning the lottery.

Grey skies. Grey sidewalk. Grey cars flying by. I dodged being splashed from a tire slashing into a puddle and turned onto a side street. Lightning cut through the sky. A neon sign in front of a variety store advertised a large lottery jackpot. Lightning flashed again. The lights in the variety store went out. I recalculated the odds and quickened my pace. Rainwater began to penetrate down into my skin.

I turned another corner. The entire block was in darkness. I was now running as quickly as I could. But my completely soaked clothes were weighing me down. When I turned onto the street leading to my apartment building, there was a woman standing in front. She was small in the distance and huddled against the rain. Last year, I would have wondered why she didn't go in out of the rain. But this year, my investigative curiosity was restricted to paperwork.

Half way down the block, I could see that the woman was short with dark hair. Long and very wet black hair. Half of me wanted to help her. The other half was weighed down from my waterlogged sweats and wanted only to be under a warm shower. I slowed down to a half jog to conserve energy.

Lightning flashed. She looked familiar. But her back was to me. All my muscles called for me to stop, to let them rest. But I was in the last mile of the marathon. I had to keep going. I *had* to—

The woman turned around. The whole street lit up. It was Jennifer! I ran to her. As fast as I could. Thunder crashed the moment I touched her.

Chapter 15

They hugged in the midst of the storm's fury, spinning themselves into the heart of the raging maelstrom. But lightning could not separate them, nor could thunder dissuade them.

When Jennifer's feet were back on the ground and she'd recovered, at least a little, from his spinning hug, she opened her mouth to speak.

But Keith pressed his finger to her lips. "Shushhh. It's wonderful to see you again. So, so wonderful! Please don't say anything. I just want to stay in the moment."

She nodded and smiled. It was all she wanted as well. They stayed there, hugging, for several minutes. Rain flowed into and through her hair, but below she was protected by a rain jacket. A rivulet trickled down his back.

Someone brushing past them drew them into the lobby.

They rode the elevator to his apartment holding hands. Once the door was shut behind him, he looked down at his bedraggled sweats. "I need a shower."

Jennifer was still smiling. "Yes, yes, you do." They were still holding hands.

"But I don't want to let go of you."

"How big is your shower?"

Keith looked at her, then shut his eyes, calculating. "We just might fit."

They stripped nude. Her fancy dress and frilly undergarments barely registered in his mind. Somehow he had less fat, more muscle definition. With two of them inside, the shower was cramped, but that suited them just fine; all they wanted was to be close to each other. Hot water warmed them.

The last drop of rainwater flowed down the drain. He shampooed her hair. She lathered him with soap, then bent him down to wash it off. They stayed together hugging. Neither was sexually aroused but both were in heaven. But gradually heat left the water spraying down onto them.

"I'm cold," she said, speaking what they both felt but what he was too proud to say.

"I think we've drained the water heater for the entire building."

She laughed and stepped out of the shower. They toweled

off, reluctantly breaking physical contact.

"I missed you," said Keith.

"I missed you, too."

"I thought you said that they forced you to break up with me?" His bathroom was very small. His only defence was the towel he held in front of him.

"What I said was that they were forcing me to choose." She too was completely vulnerable.

"But you're here."

"But I'm here."

They stood nervously, holding their towels.

She shivered. Cold. Had it been a mistake to come here?

"I have a blanket," he offered.

"On your bed?" There was hope in her voice, but she dared only expose a hint of it.

He nodded. "And sheets."

They fumbled in the bathroom so that he could shift around her and lead her to the bedroom. He pulled back the covers. She scampered underneath. He stood, waiting.

She smiled up at him. "Aren't you coming in?"

He didn't need a second invitation. They cuddled in the small bed, letting their bodies warm each other.

After a while, he decided to take another chance. "You said that they were forcing you to choose."

"Uh, uh," she nodded, enjoying the feel of her cheek against his chest.

"And?" Keith had stepped to the ledge. Now she had to answer. He was filled with hope and dread.

She lifted her head and stared deeply into his eyes. "I came here."

Smiles spread across their lips. "Lie back," he said.

She did and he began to lightly run his hand over her body. He was barely touching, but she quivered nonetheless. He avoided her head, breasts and pubic areas. She opened her mouth to beg to be touched everywhere, but he kissed her on the lips. The kiss was so light she barely felt its touch, but it tingled down her spine. She sighed, shut her eyes and relaxed into his finger lingering over her belly button, tracing circles 'round its rim.

This was vanilla sex at its finest, she reflected. And Keith was the epitome of vanilla—safe, secure, erring on the side of bland.

Maybe too vanilla, but maybe that's what I need.

His fingers on her breasts, circling towards her nipples brought Jennifer back to the here and now. She gasped as he touched the upper edge of her nipples.

"Flick my barbells," she told him.

"Are you sure?"

She nodded.

He flicked.

Jennifer winced, half pain, half ecstasy. She reached up, pulled him down to her lips, established secure suction and circled her tongue around the edge of his mouth. His tongue touched hers and they moaned into each other's cheeks.

She felt his hands flutter down to her tummy and their kiss intensified. This time he didn't avoid her pubic region but instead pushed his fingers over her mound. One touched her clit, its electricity drawing her sex towards his hand. Her head jerked away from him—she had to breathe!

Keith lifted his leading finger up as his other fingers slid down the sides of her vulva. His eyes stared into hers, possessing her, and Jennifer demanded that he keep her forever. His lead finger came down again, but this time it was at the bottom of her vagina.

"You're wet," he told her.

"And warm."

"Very warm."

"And inviting."

His finger took the invitation and she trembled, ever so slightly. "More," she pleaded.

He slipped his finger all the way in, then pulled it back. Her breath caught halfway. He stroked in and out. "More," she pleaded.

Jennifer gasped as he inserted a second finger, then moaned as he continued his stroking. Her pelvis pressed upward, trying to push him further inside. "Keith," she pleaded.

He withdrew his fingers and swung himself up and over her, his body aligned with hers, readying to mount her. He bent down to kiss her. The kiss was long and wet. The tip of his penis throbbed against her pussy lips. He parted her hips and began to rock his hips to aid in his penetration—

But Jennifer twirled. Now instead of being head to head, her tongue cavorting with his cock, her tongue licked the bottom of his balls. He shuddered, emboldening her to suck one of his balls halfway into her mouth.

She heard him moan, then felt his fingers on her hips, then his hands grip and pull her sex towards him. Her tongue flickered along his cock, then lost contact. His mouth enveloped her, arching her back.

Keith licked up and down her pussy. Occasionally he sucked, but ever so lightly. His tongue lacked plan and pattern, but he was enthusiastic and his flicks and licks constantly varied their angle, pressure and duration.

Jennifer repeatedly tried to kiss his cock, but their relative sizes made this impossible. All she could do was touch him, but that wasn't quite the same. Equally frustrating was the fact that his tonguing, while extremely pleasant, wasn't quite enough to allow her to climax. She repeatedly felt tingles tickle the bottom of her spine and clenched herself to encourage the contractions which would signal orgasm, but her efforts only pushed the tingles back down into her sex.

She squirmed and Keith got the signal that he should try to mount her again. He twisted around and kissed her. She tasted herself. It wasn't unpleasant, but it wasn't sexy either. He positioned himself for penetration but Jennifer shook her head.

"I'm too wet for missionary," she told him.

"But—"

"Let's try from the rear."

She knelt on the bed, elevating her butt high in the air. He shuffled around behind her and fumbled to find her opening. Jennifer gripped his cock and guided him in. She was tight, but so lubricated that he slid in easily. He thrust in and out, slapping himself against her thighs.

Again, Keith stimulated her to the cusp of orgasm, but his thrusts were somehow not quite enough to push her over the edge. Worse, she felt him floating, his hands barely touching her hips. It would take only a little more of this to milk his life force into her and send him collapsing onto the bed next to her.

She extended herself forward and he popped out.

"Sorry," he mumbled, trying to reestablish penetration.

But she flopped onto her back. "Let's try a leg wrap," she said.

He looked at her as if she'd proposed an outing for fast food.

She laughed and raised her legs up off the bed, her knees

bent at ninety degrees. "Lie beside me," she directed, "and enter from the side."

After much fumbling and giggling, he succeeded in entering her. He stroked dutifully. But his head was above hers and he was looking sideways. She had no idea what he was feeling. She wished she were taller. His cock felt good down below, really good, but she wanted more.

Jennifer scooted forward and was finally able to kiss him, or rather sort of kiss him as their mouths were sideways to each other. But once again, Keith's cock flopped out of her. They laughed, kissed and tickled each other.

In a moment, they were out of breath and facing each other sideways on the bed, his cock between her legs. She raised her left leg. "Let's try a scissor," she suggested.

More fumbling and giggling ensued but finally, he had had his lower leg over hers and her upper leg entwined around it. At first, he was barely inside her, but when his penetration moved their legs into proper position, they managed to bring their pubic bones together.

She felt Keith's cock fill her and his leg rub most pleasantly up and down her vulva. *This was more like it!* He had to work hard to stroke in and out, reducing his sensation while maximizing hers. Occasionally he bent to kiss her and their chests rubbed together.

"This is nice," she said.

"Very."

"You feel good inside me."

He grunted, his exertions requiring all his energy. She smiled and played with his chest, teasing his concentration back down to between their pelvises.

Jennifer felt an orgasm begin to organize itself within her. But she sensed that he was some distance away. She scooted upwards, onto her back, pulling him out of her. Frustration flickered across his face but it immediately vanished when she spread her legs. "Now, Keith," she implored.

He climbed atop her and gently entered. She was no longer wet and he tugged at her genitals as he thrust inside. The pressure lessened as he pulled out, but other sensations made up for the lack of pressure. A twinge danced halfway up her spine. She gasped.

"Are you alright?" he asked, slowing the pace of his strokes.

"Never better! Now give it to me. Fast and hard!"

Keith grunted. He slammed himself in. She thrusted upwards, matching his power. Her eyes shut. He felt her sheath wrap tightly around the fleshy knife with which he was impaling her. Jenny was so hot—down there, her chest, her entire body! She started to thrash around the bed. But he grasped her buttocks tight pulling her into him. Still she thrashed. He was determined not to let himself flop out again so he rested his entire weight against her.

Now she couldn't move, except an inch or two between their legs. But still she wiggled violently.

"Jesus!" she cried.

"Jennifer?"

"Harder!"

He stroked harder. He wouldn't be able to hold on much longer.

"Harder! Faster!" she screamed.

He mashed himself into her. She quivered around him.

"Harder! Faster!"

Keith felt her contract around his pole.

"Jesus!" she yelled.

Jennifer was no longer thrashing about so he lifted himself off her. Her hips rocked him in and out of her at a furious pace.

"Give it to me!" she yelled.

He thrust into her as hard and as fast as he could. Her contractions were dissipating and she was breathing again. She looked up at him, a dreamy look in her eyes.

His spine jerked taut. She'd felt it too.

"Fuck me, Keith Martin. Fuck me good."

"I—"

"No words. No thinking. Just fucking." The gleam in her eyes was so feral, it was almost evil.

He grunted. It was all about him. She'd already reached her climax. She moved her hips sideways. He spasmed to a stop. She squeezed and squeezed—with each squeeze she felt him pump himself into her. Spurt after spurt after spurt. Only when there was nothing left to spurt could he move again. They stroked him in and out of her, grasping at the last strands of the pleasure of their lovemaking.

After he'd recovered his breath, he pulled himself out of her and collapsed noisily down beside her.

"That was wonderful," he told her.

"It truly was!" She lifted herself up and over him and planted a kiss on his lips, chuckling at his nostrils fighting to keep oxygen flowing.

An hour later, they ate French fries across his kitchen table.

"Will I see you…?" he ventured.

"I'm sure you will."

He smiled and popped a ketchup-laden fry into his mouth.

But, she thought to herself, *next time it'll be more adventurous.*

The End

Backnotes

Thank you for reading this story. If you enjoyed it, **please** take a moment to **post a review**.

Other Stories by Jason Pinaster

Stories featuring Mistress Megan:
Pro Dom Her First Client
Pro Dom 2 Hugo
Pro Dom 3 Cross Dresser
Pro Dom 4 Hugo & Sheila
Pro Dom 5 Cold
Pro Dom 6 Lucas Comes Again
Pro Dom 7 Walk-in
Pro Dom 8 Womyn
Pro Dom 9 Priest
Pro Dom 10 Cocoon
Pro Dom 11 Outcall
Pro Dom 12 Switch

Other Recent Stories
Tickle Test
Pay Back
Panty Play
Webcam Spank
Tiebreaker (A SleeperKidsWorld.com story)
Couples: Adventures at Hedonism II
Gunge Girl
Squished
The Prize
Ava's WAM
Sex Wrestler
WAM Mix (a wet and messy story)
Truth be Dared

Spank Me—if you Dare!

The Lusty Lee Logs:
Available in one convenient volume
Lusty Lee: The Entire Logs:
From Prequel to Confronting
Or separately
Prequel Lusty Lee Log #00
The Case, Lusty Lee Log #1
Swinging, Lusty Lee Log #2
Strip Club, Lusty Lee Log #3
The Escort, Lusty Lee Log #4
Leather, Lusty Lee Log #5
Lusty Lee Box Set 1: Prequel through Log 5
Hedonism, Lusty Lee Log #6
Hedo II, Lusty Lee Log #7
Cheaters, Lusty Lee Log #8
The Actor, Lusty Lee Log #9
Yearning, Lusty Lee Log #10
Lusty Lee Box Set 2: Logs 6 thru 10 and 7a
Scandal, Lusty Lee Log 11
Michael, Lusty Lee Log 12
Rumballs, Lusty Lee Log 13
Massage, Lusty Lee Log 14
The Aide, Lusty Lee Log 15
Lusty Lee Box Set 3: Logs 11 through 16
Negotiator, Lusty Lee Log 16
Linebacker, Lusty Lee Log 17
Cosplay, Lusty Lee Log 18
Wrestling, Lusty Lee Log 19
Anger, Lusty Lee Log 20
Lusty Lee Box Set 4: Logs 17 through 20
Cops, Lusty Lee Log 21
Paintball, Lusty Lee Log 22
Interrogation, Lusty Lee Log 23

I Alien Vacation, a novelette

II **Connie's Crop, a novel**
Wherein mild-mannered Marsha pursuit of the magical whip pairs her with sexy Sheila and connects her with the darker side of sexuality.

III **The Christopher Carter Series**

Carter's Chance II
Private Party His
Private Party Hers
Private Party Box Set
Ryan's Reprieve
Cashmere Congress
Melissa's Moxie
Molly Madness
Melissa's Memories
Blackmail Bounce
Assisting Audrey
Splosh Scoundrel (my most popular splosh story)
Jody's Journal
Busted Bonds
Solicitor's Slip
Stakeout Story

Aural Artifact
Mayan Magic
Party Photos
Buying Before
Cardiac Caress
Credit Card Con
Formatting Foam
Clinic Caper
Cosplay Clue
Witch's Wrath
Carter's Climax Box Set*: All 25 stories*

And please check out my author profiles at
http://www.amazon.com/Jason-
Pinaster/e/B00YSLUDNG/ref=sr_tc_2_0?qid=1434908188&
sr=1-2-ent   and at
https://www.smashwords.com/profile/view/JasonPinaster

For more adventurous versions of the covers, follow me
on Pinterest: https://www.pinterest.com/jasonpinaster/

Cheers!

Jason Pinaster

www.ingramcontent.com/pod-product-compliance
Lightning Source LLC
Chambersburg PA
CBHW030345180626
46812CB00007B/2771